MW01701997

Sin 4 Life

A Novel By
Parish M. Sherman

SKP

Street Knowledge Publishing LLC
Website: www.streetknowledgepublication.com
Myspace: www.myspace.com/streetknowledgepublishing

Published by: **Street Knowledge Publishing** Written by: Parish M.Sherman Edited by: Dolly Lopez Cover design by: Marion Designs/ www.mariondesigns.com Photos by: Marion Designs

For information contact:
Street Knowledge Publishing
P.O. Box Box 345
Wilmington, DE 19801
Email: jj@streetknowledgepublishing.com
Website: www.streetknowledgepublishing.com
Myspace: www.myspace.com/streetknowledgepublishing

ISBN: 0-9746199-8-1

Dedication

This book is dedicated to those that inspired me in the game. Some are no longer with us and others are still making noise in the town (Oakland, California) one way or another. First and foremost my Father Michael Wayne Sherman Sr. I love and miss you. I know if you were still alive I would either not have anything to do with the game or I would have mastered it. My uncle Ray E. Coleman. You were called up at a young age, but you lived a fuller life than mutha fuckas that are the age you would have been had you still been alive. Next is the undisputed king of the town, Felix Mitchel. You did your thang like no other in the town's history. You all may be gone, but you're not forgotten. Rest in peace.

Now my living dedications: Anthony "A.L." Livingston, Darryl "Lil D" Reed, Black, Ant Flowers. Hillbilly, Phil, D.D., James "Hollyrock" Holloway, Gary Lloyd, Mickey & June Moe, Shelia Big Harv, and my nigga DoRod.

Acknowledgment

I have to thank God for creating my parents who in turn created me. I would like to thank my moms Jackie Nash for having my back on whatever. My brothers, Pastor Demorie Sherman and Shaheed Nkosi. D, man when I was young I wanted to be like you. You was the flyest cat I had ever known. I'm glad you got saved and followed the Lord. For real what you said to me on the phone was on point. You were way more wilder than me and Shaheed and we're the ones that got caught up. My brother Shaheed, dude you the realest mutha fucka I've ever known. You touched down from doing that dime and ain't looked back. I'm going to start calling you Shaheed Trump, because that real estate thing you putting down is something serious. You ain't had to kill them like that with the CLS500 like you did. **THAT'S MY BROTHER and HIS CAR ON THE COVER OF THIS BOOK!** My cousin Petria "Moonie" Sherman. Moons you like a big sister to me. When my moms booted me up out the joint you looked out for me. I'm proud of you too. You had a minor slip and you bounced back. I love you, cuzzo. I gotta thank the three people that made this shit possible. This ain't in no particular order. Whaida Clark, you are by far my favorite author. You are the true Queen of Hip Hop fiction. Thank you for reading my stuff and encouraging me to push it. I know I was suppose to been had it done. You are truly a jewel in the game. Darrell DeBrew. You looked at my stuff also and gave me pointers and then turned me on to the realest chick in this game. I'm forever grateful, dawg.

Linda Williams. What can I say about you? You are the realest like I just said. Without your pushing I would have still been writing to pass time. You got me my deal, you did my typing, you send me books, and you give me good advice. There aren't enough thank you's in the world I can say to add up to what you mean to me and this project. You are by far a blessing to me and everyone you help. Thank you again. All my friends and fam that wasn't mentioned I'll hit you off in part two.

A Message From the Author

I want to leave everyone with something to think about. The game ain't to be won. White folks the only ones winning in the game. We ain't bringing that dope over here. We ain't the ones making the guns. We don't own the diamond mines or the Dialmer Chrysler Corporation. For you all that don't know that's who own the Mercedes Company. So mutha fuckas out there really hustling in the game for the white folks that do own those companies. Because that's what we buying with the loot, feel me?

In every circle there's a weak link. I don't give a fuck who you are or where you from. Somebody you fuck with is telling, has told, or will tell. The game ain't what it used to be. The saying on the street now is "Get off before you get got off on." Which means tell first. I don't know how people do it in other places, but where I'm from snitches don't get stitches. Nah, they bitch asses get found in ditches. By no means am I telling anyone to go dome a snitch. Game recognizes game though and read between the lines.

I appreciate you reading this book and I know it leaves you hanging. It will pick up exactly where it left off in part two "A Little More Sin." I would like to hear comments from the readers. Dudes the in Yay Area where I'm from getting it like Sin and his folks.

Rest In Peace Mac Dre

Write the Author at:
Parish Sherman 13080-097
Unit A4A-30L
P.O. Box 7001
Taft, California 93268

Chapter One

Shaunté

"I don't give a fuck about that shit! The only thing I give a fuck about is getting my muthafuckin' money right," Shaunté said angrily.

"I'm saying, what the fuck you expect me to do? I can't make this cat give me that shit!" Jumani said slightly raising his voice.

Shaunté looked at him disgusted. "You 'bout a coward muthafucka!"

Shaunté was 5'7", 118 pounds, had long, silky sandy brown hair, copper colored skin, and tight light brown eyes. She had big 36D titties, a small waist, wide sexy hips, nice sexy shapely thighs, and a nice sized round butt. She was dime by anyone's standards. No one would ever think that encased in all that beauty was a straight killer. She was 26 years old and had been in the fast life since she was 13. She had boosted clothes, stolen cars, committed strong arm robberies, pimped, and even sold her own ass when times were really hard. She found the dope game more lucrative.

She ran a crew of four chicks and three guys, and that was going to be minus one guy because he didn't have the balls *she* needed. She looked to her two lieutenants, Lisa and Déja, standing behind Jumani. Lisa and Shaunté had been friends since kindergarten. Déja hooked up with them in 7th grade. They had always been about their money.

"Déja, bring that sucka ass nigga Willie B to me!" Shaunté said. Déja turned and left.

"Your punk ass fired! Leave that gun and keys to the spot," she said to Jumani.

"Hold on, man! You tripping!" Jumani pleaded.

"Punk ass nigga, who the fuck you talking to? You heard what the fuck she said!" Lisa said from her position behind him with the 9mm Glock in her hand.

Lisa was top notch too. She was 5'9", 124 pounds, with long silky black hair. She was toffee colored, had brown eyes, and had a cute face with a sexy mole on the top lip of her sexy mouth. Her body was something else. She had a tiny 20-inch waist, wide hips, sexy EnVouge thighs, a flat stomach, nice sized 36C titties, and major ass.

Jumani sighed as he took the keys out his pocket and put them on the desk. He then pulled the gun out and handed it to Shaunté with the barrel down. Jumani gave Shaunté and Lisa a crazy look and walked out.

"That nigga a straight bitch," Lisa said as she sat down in the chair in front of the desk.

"And to think, I was going to give him some pussy," Shaunté said.

"Speaking of which, I gotta date with this Hayward nigga with a hurricane tongue," Lisa said.

"I don't know how you do it. I be wanting my back blown out," Shaunté said. She hadn't had sex in the last three months because she hadn't been really attracted to the dudes that were getting at her.

"I just let these marks give me a cool tongue lashing then send them on their way. I'm only letting worthy muthafuckas in, and as it stands, ain't too many around," Lisa said.

"You ain't never lied," Shaunté said as she and Lisa slapped five.

"Tay, don't have Déja bring Willie over here. You gon' end up going off and letting that nigga have it up in here," Lisa said, using Shaunté's nickname as she picked up her purse.

"Leave your phone on," Shaunté said. Lisa nodded as she left.

Damn, I need a man! I can't get down with this casual sex shit, Shaunté thought. She picked up the phone and called Déja and told her to just wait for her on the block. Shaunté picked the gun up and put it in her purse. She stood in front of the full length mirror and looked at herself. She had to admit she was working the short blue denim Prada skirt that came to high-thigh, the matching jacket, and the over-the knee-high heeled black leather boots. She grabbed her keys and left. When she got outside she got into her new cream colored 1998 Lexus LS400 and pushed the remote to the stereo. LSG's hit *My Body* came on pounding. Shaunté threw the car in gear and mashed off.

When Shaunté pulled up on Bromly, she parked down the street from her spot. Déja got out her 97 Camaro and got into the Lexus.

"He's sitting next door to our spot on the porch."

Déja was 5'7" and 120 pounds. She was dark chocolate colored, and had a short Halle Berry cut, gray eyes, and she was as thick as they came. She had 34DD titties that didn't sag, a 22-

inch waist, wide hips and a gang of ass. She liked girls as much as she liked boys. Shaunté had been tempted a few times but was scared to approach her.

They both cocked their guns and got out the car and proceeded down the street. Shaunté noticed how Déja's ass bounced under the short school girl skirt. *I really need a man.* When Willie B looked up and saw them coming up the walkway he stood up quick.

"Nigga you even *think* about running or reaching, I'm melting your punk ass," Shaunté hissed. Willie B froze up.

"Sh… Sh... Shaunté! What's all this for?" he stuttered. Willie B had a gun in his pants, but knew the chances of him pulling it before either one the females squeezed the trigger was slim to none. Déja walked behind him and put her 45 to his head. She then reached around him and stripped him of his gun.

"Nigga, you got my muthafuckin 5 gees?" Shaunté asked quietly.

Willie thought fast. "I'll have it tomorrow," he pleaded. Shaunté looked at Déja, who now had two guns on Willie.

"Where the dope at, and empty your fuckin' pockets," Shaunté said. Willie B sighed with relief. He was going to live. He had $2,500 in his pocket and $1,000.00 in rocks in the bushes. She would never see the other $1,500. He was going to get in the wind with that.

"The money's in my coat pocket and the dope is in that bag in the bush over there," Willie said.

Shaunté nodded at Déja. Déja went through Willie's

pockets and grabbed the money. She then bent over and grabbed the dope out the bush.

Willie turned and ran knocking Déja down. He ran down the path on the side of the house. Shaunté started getting off at him and Déja started busting both guns. Right before Willie got to the back he was hit in the shoulder and the neck.

"Come on, we gotta bounce!" Shaunté said as she helped Déja up.

She grabbed the money and hurried down the street to her car. She jumped in the Lexus and smashed off. Shaunté pulled her phone out when she got to Seminary and MacArthur and called Déja.

"What's up?" Déja answered.

"You a'ight?" Shaunté asked.

"I'm good. What you want me to do?" Shaunté loved that about Déja. She didn't give a damn. Anything that needed to be done, she did. She was down for whatever.

"Just go change clothes and cars and post up and see what the police do. If they don't go behind the spot and find the body, go get Boogie and have him steal a truck and ya'll clean that shit up."

"A'ight" Déja said and hung up.

Shaunté decided to go hit the club and peep the dudes. She might find her a man. If not, she would just pull a "Lisa" and take somebody to the motel and let them give her head all night.

She took the 98th avenue exit and rode down to MacArthur and bent a left and rode until she got to the Sports Page. The Ballers were in full swing. There were S600's, Range Rovers, Navigators, 'Vettes, BMW's and Lexus' everywhere. There were also guys out there in old schools from the 60 and 70 era. *I'm going to buy me a old school, s*he thought. Shaunté parked around the corner and walked back. All kinds of cats were at her. These were the same dudes that had been at her, and she wasn't interested.

Chapter Two

Sin

Simian Michaels, better known as Sin, looked out the window of the airplane as it touched the ground at Oakland International Airport. The last time he was there was four years ago when he took off to Atlanta on one of his weekly trips that ended up all bad. Sin had just spent the last four years in a Georgia State Prison. He was happy to finally be home. He lucked up on this case. By rights he was still suppose to be locked up. He spent a grip on a good lawyer, and instead of getting the thirty-one years they were trying to give him, he walked away with four.

Sin was riding through College Park on his way to meet the guy he was about to make a five key sale to, Mike, when he got pulled over for not using his blinker. The police searched the car and found a Glock 40. They took him straight to jail and impounded the Dodge Intrepid rental car and did a thorough search and found the five kilos of cocaine. By the car being a rental and the dope being stashed the way it was, the prosecutor couldn't prove the dope was Sin's. His fingerprints were on the gun, so he took the deal for four years.

Sin still had over $50,000.00 when he went to prison. His girl, Yvette, ran off with another dude and took two of his three cars, the jewels, and his money. Sin was very bitter. His brother Erick III, a-k-a June Bug, whom was having big money, didn't send him a dime. June looked out for Sin's kids though. The only people that looked out for Sin were his mom, and his son's mom, Tracy. Tracy was with another dude, but she still brought the kids to see Sin twice a year, sent him packages and like $100 a month. Tracy might have lived with ol' boy, but she still looked out for the one she loved.

As Sin was walking through the airport he caught his reflection in a window. When he went to jail he was 24 years old, 6'3", 175 pounds, slim built, caramel colored, and had long braids. He was now a couple shades darker, 200 pounds, solid build and had a bald head. He always thought he had average looks even though women always said he was fine. He walked out of the airport and stood there waiting for his moms.

"Daddy!" he heard a voice yell. He looked to his left and saw he and Tracy's son, Malik, leaning out the gray 97 Camry. Sin grinned as he walked up to the car and pulled his 7-year-old twin out and hugged him. Malik Simian Michaels. They nicknamed him Busy because he was always moving when Tracy was pregnant with him. They got in the car and he looked for his daughter.

"Where's Quesha?" he asked as he looked at Tracy. He knew he made a mistake by leaving her.

"She's at your mom's. You got a little darker," Tracy said and leaned over and kissed him on the mouth. "Welcome home." She started the car and pulled off. Sin kissed her cheek.

"Thanks for looking out like you did. I mean the money, the visits, and taking care of Quesha," he said.

Quesha's mom, Kesha, was on dope bad. Sin had custody of Quesha and even when he and Tracy broke up, she stayed with Tracy and took to calling her mama. Tracy reached over and squeezed his hand.

"All I did was play my part like *you* taught me, and as far as Marquesha goes, that's my little girl," she said.

Sin kept staring at Tracy. At 26 Tracy was looking better

than Sin had ever thought possible. She was cocoa brown colored, had brown eyes, long black braids, and an earring in her nose. She was beautiful for real. Everyone said she looked like the singer Brandy, but with a body. She stood at 5'11" and weighed 135 pounds. What caught Sin's eye when he and Tracy met was her body. She was wearing a short, tight low cut green dress which had her 38C titties, wide hips, long sexy legs and thighs, and big round ass looking right. There were a gang of dudes in the club sweating her but she kept brushing them off. Sin walked over to her and grabbed her hand and pulled her away from the vultures, and it was on from there.

Tracy didn't sleep with Sin for close to two months after they met because he was with Kesha. During that time they spent nights together, and at 5:00 every morning Sin slid out the bed and hit the freeway to Vallejo where he and Kesha lived. When Sin and Kesha broke up he moved in with Tracy. It was on for real.

"What's up? You with me tonight?" he asked. Tracy started laughing. As much as she wanted to she knew Sin would never do the 9 to 5 thing, the game had him.

"Nope. I'm not going to do Brian like that. If he was fucking up there would be no question to where I would be going. Before I forget, here," she said as she handed him some money.

"What's this?" Sin asked.

"That's $1,000, a piece of my income tax return. I know you ain't about to sit still. When you're back on top don't forget about the one who's had your back the last eight years."

"I'd rather be back on top of you," he said.

"Baby, I know. I'm not into dogging people out. I didn't do it to you, I'm not going to do it to him. Anyway, Brian's crazy. I don't want anything to happen to either one of us" she said and laughed.

"You already know how I get down. I'll have that fool's head," Sin said.

"Oh, yeah? Here," Tracy said trying to change the subject. She handed him a new Motorola Star-Tac cellular phone.

"When I get back to something nice I'm gon' break you off something cool," he said.

When they pulled up at this mom's North Oakland home he saw his 1992 Chevy K5 blazer sitting there, sparkling. The truck was midnight blue with chrome flakes in the paint, with six coats of glass over it for the shine. Sin put four 15"' EV woofers, JVC mids tweeters, and 6x9's in it along with a JVC Deck with CD changer with remote. He topped it off with two 600 watt Zeus amps and a talking Invaisibeam alarm system. Yvette really did a number on him. She got the money, the Benz, and the brand new 1994 drop Camaro Z-28.

"That punk ass bitch really fucked you over. I saw her and that dude she married at Hot August Nights, in *your* Benz. They didn't even have the decency to paint it. Everybody up there knew it was yours. It's the only white 500 with the green pearl in the paint around. I told you not to put your stuff in her name," Tracy said.

"You been paying the insurance on the Benz, right?" he asked. Tracy nodded.

"As soon as I see that bitch, I'm burning that car up. The

insurance is a down payment on another one," Sin said. Tracy just shook her head.

"You still in love with that bitch," she said.

"Fuck that hoe! All she was good for was licking my ass," he said.

They went to the door and went in. Sin's mom looked up and saw him. "Simian!" she screamed and hurried to him. Sin hugged his mom. Jackie Michaels had lived a hard life, but looking at her you wouldn't be able to tell. At 49 she could still pass for 30. She worked for The phone company since she was 18. When she met Erick Michaels Jr., A-K-A Junior, it was love at first sight.

Erick had two other kids by another woman. One was Jasmine, whom they nicknamed Jazz, and Erick III. When Sin was 2 Jackie had another baby, Kim. Jazz and June Bug's mom, Dahlylah, died when Jazz was 9 and June Bug was 7. They came to live with Jackie. Jackie treated them like her own. At that time Sin was 4 and Kim was 2.

Junior went on the run from the Feds in 1982 leaving Jackie to raise four kids. Jazz had got pregnant by a major player in the dope game, Gary Jackson, and she left home to live with him at age 15. June Bug at the age of 14 stepped up to be the man of the house. He got a whiff of the dope game and it was on ever since.

Jackie started working two jobs so she could move her two remaining kids out the notorious 20's in East Oakland.

She saw how 12-year-old Simian was mirroring June Bug's ways. When Sin turned 14 he slid into the game too. Sin and a few cats he went to school with hooked up and started getting wild. They called themselves The Mad Circle. Out of all of them, the ones that bubbled to the top were, Scatter, Tariq, Amir, Eddie, Hasahn, Sin's cousin Lil' Rod, and D-Boy, who had gotten killed at the young age of 17.

In the beginning Sin only hated one person, and that was his father, Junior. Junior never once came back or called, and as far as Sin was concerned he was a bitch. Back then the Mad Circle consisted of cats from all over East, West, and North Oakland. Now they had cats in Richmond, Pittsburg, and Sacramento. They were now close to 50 plus deep.

Sin was hugging his mom when his 9-year-old daughter, Marquesha, came out.

"Daddy!" she screamed and came and hugged him. Sin bent down and kissed her. Quesha was a carbon copy of her mom. She was bright skinned with freckles, long black hair, and dark brown eyes. She was tall for 9, and slim. The only things she inherited from Sin were her smile and good hair. Malik on the other hand inherited everything from Sin.

Sin kicked it with his family for a while then Tracy took the kids home. Sin went to his old room and pulled a foot locker from under the bed and stuck a key in it and opened it. He pulled a .45 automatic out. He locked the locker and slid it back up under the bed. *It's time for these suckas to pay they bills.* He went out the back door and went and got in his truck. He pulled off knocking Richie Rich. His destination was the East.

When Sin turned on Havenscourt and Bancroft he saw J.J. *This just the muthafucka I was looking for.* He parked across the street from T-Wauzi records and watched J.J. make 15 sales. Sin cocked the 45 and slid it in his coat as he got out. He crept up on

J.J. while his back was turned and stuck the 45 in his ribs.

"Let me holla at you, Potna," he said as he looked around to make sure no one was paying attention. He pushed J.J. around the corner of some apartments.

"Nigga, what's up with that $3,500 you owe me?" Sin asked as he put the gun to J.J.'s head. J.J. was spooked.

"Sin, I swear I'm gon' pay you!" he said.

"What you got on you?" Sin asked as he pulled the 9mm out of J.J.'s waistband and pushed him away.

"Like 2 gees," he said.

"Let me get that, and since you wanna be talking about I ain't got nothing coming, you still owe me $3,500," Sin said as he pocketed the money.

"I'll have it tomorrow," J.J. said.

"Tell Jerry and Sammy I'm looking for them, and they would want to come holla at me before I catch up with them," Sin said as he took the clip out of J.J.'s gun and threw it in the bushes and walked away. J.J. let out a long breath. He knew he just cheated death. He would make sure he paid Sin. That other $3,500 wasn't worth his life.

●●●●●●

Alonzo and his cousin Jeff were sitting in the Sports Page having a drink and plotting.

"It's big bread up in here tonight. Pick which one we gon'

jack," Jeff said. Alonzo looked around just as Shaunté was coming in.

"Her right there. That's at least 25 gees, and it should be easy," he said as he watched Shaunté speak to Rodney Jackson who was by far one of the five richest dudes in the club.

"Cuzzo, if that broad hooked up with The Circle, we need to give her a pass. Rod, June, and Scatter ain't like these suckas." Jeff said. Alonzo looked at his cousin.

"Man, I feel you, but I ain't scared of them niggas. Fuck all them Mad Circle niggas!" he said.

●●●●●●

Sin stepped in the club and saw Rod and June sitting at a corner table. He saw June's right hand man, Kiaree, sitting at the table to the left and Rod's boy, Cedric, at the table to the right. He ordered a Remy XO and was greeted by a couple of cats and broads he knew. Rod looked up as Sin was walking up.

"Sin, what up, Cuzzo!" Rod said and hugged him.

"I didn't know you was getting out today," June said. Sin looked at June Bug.

"Nigga, that's how you carrying it?" Sin asked. June sipped his XO and looked at Sin.

"Nigga, maybe you forgot. Three of them birds you got caught with was mine. I lost $45,000 on that," June said. Sin wanted to get on his brother bad. He just shook his head.

"Nigga, you need to quit this hater ass shit you be with.

You trick 45,000 off with them stanking ass bitches you be fucking with." Sin looked at Rod.

"Cuzzo, I got $2,500. Can I get some come up?"

"Keep your money. I got something for you. Call me in the morning," he said. Sin killed his drink and walked away.

●●●●●●

Shaunté saw Sin when he came in. She watched him get his drink and walk over and hug Rod. *Damn! I wonder who that is.* Sin walked away and he caught Shaunté eye. *Oh yeah, some new work,* Shaunté thought.

●●●●●●

Damn, who's she? Sin made his way towards Shaunté. *Oh yeah, I'm at that for sho,* Sin thought.

"What's up with you, lil' mama?" he asked standing in front of her.

"Nothing, what's up with you?" *Damn, this nigga's fine!*

"You believe in love at first sight?" Sin asked as he sized her up. *I'm hittin' these tonight.*

"Is that what I'm feeling?" Shaunté asked and giggled.

"Naw, Boo that's what *I'm* feeling," Sin said and smiled at her.

"Baby, you gonna sit down, or I gotta keep looking up at you?" she asked.

Sin signaled one of the waitresses and sat down. “What’s up, Sin?” Dottie asked as she walked up.

“Give me another XO, and give her whatever she wants,” he said. Dottie looked at Shaunté.

“I’ll have the same,” Shaunté said. Dottie walked away. “I’m Shaunté,” she said as if he was supposed to know the name.

“I’m Sin. Shaunté, where your dude at,” he asked.

“I don’t have one. I’m happily single,” she said. They sat there and talked until the club started emptying out.

“You with me tonight?” he asked as he stood up and stretched.

“Where we going?” she asked.

“Motel 6 on the Embarcadero.”

“I’ll meet you there,” she said. She stood up and grabbed her purse. When Sin turned around he saw someone who he had been dreaming of putting his hands on for the last four years… Yvette.

Yvette was still fine. Five feet-9”, 140 pounds, long dyed blond hair, high yellow complexion, and dark brown eyes. She had 38C titties, and a gang of ass. Shaunté saw the evil look on Sin’s face.

“I’ll meet you by the door,” he said as he walked off. When he got close to Yvette’s table, her friend, Myesha, saw him first and got bug-eyed.

"Ooohhh shit!" she said. Yvette turned and saw Sin and the color drained from her face.

"Bitch, you must have thought I had life! Have my shit at my mom's house in the morning or I'm killing you. Test me if you want to." Shaunté took that moment to walk up.

"Sin, we up outta here or what?" she asked as she looked crazy at Yvette and her potna.

"Yeah, we out. Bitch, play with me if you want to," he said as he put his arm around Shaunté and walked out the club.

"Who was that?" she asked.

"I'll tell you later."

They walked around the corner to Shaunté's Lexus. Sin's truck was parked a little further down the street. Sin saw a dude with a ski mask on across the street.

"What the fuck?" he said and pulled his gun out. Shaunté was reaching in her purse and coming out with her gun when they heard the distinct sound of somebody cocking an AK.

"Sin, both ya'll put that shit down," a voice said from behind them. They looked, and he was also wearing a mask. The dude across the street stepped out pointing the Mac 11.

Sin and Shaunté both lay down their guns.

"Empty ya pockets," the other dude said. Sin recognized the dude's squeaky voice. *That's that nigga Jeff! I bet the other fool's is that sucka Alonzo. I can't let them niggas know I know who they are or I'm dead*, he thought.

"Break ya self," Alonzo said. Sin took the $3,000 out of his pocket and handed it over.

"Bitch, you too," Alonzo said to Shaunté.

"Nigga, I ain't about to help you rob me," she said. He snatched her purse and got $2,500.

"Take me to the real loot," Alonzo said.

"You cats called me by my name. If you know me, you know I'm broke, and I just got out the Pen," Sin said, hoping they would let them go.

"We know we could get a mill ticket from June for your life. We ain't on that kinda time right now. We want the loot *this* bitch got," Alonzo said.

Shaunté eyes misted over. After all the hustling she did to get the money she got, these cats were stripping her for it.

"This is some bullshit!" she said.

"Follow us in our car," Alonzo said to Jeff. Jeff ran down the street. "Ya'll in front." Alonzo said. Sin and Shaunté got in the front of the Lexus and he got in the back and pulled the 9mm Beretta out and put it to Shaunté's head.

"This will be easy. Take us to the loot and we gone. You try something, *you* gone, in a box," he said.

Shaunté rolled in silence. *As soon as I see a police car, I'm slamming on my breaks so they'll pull me over.* Shaunté made it all the way to the Skyline Hills town houses without seeing one cop. *When a muthafucka need they assess they ain't nowhere to be found. If I was doing some dumb shit they'd be on my ass.*

She pushed the remote and the black wrought iron gate slid open. She pulled in and the black Buick following her pulled in behind her. Shaunté rode to the back of the complex and parked in her assigned space.

They all got out and she went to the door and opened it and deactivated the alarm. They went to the living room.

"Where's it at?" Alonzo said. Shaunté pointed to the hall closet.

"Get it," he said. She opened the closet and saw the SKS sitting there. She knew she wouldn't be able to pull it out, cock it, aim, and shoot before the two of them killed her. She grabbed the blue backpack and brought it out and tossed it at the dude's feet.

Alonzo pulled some plastic wire ties out his pocket and pointed at the dining-room chairs. "Cuzzo, tie them up," he said to Jeff. Sin and Shaunté sat down. Jeff bound their hands. He rubbed Shaunté titty as he was standing up. Shaunté had tears in her eyes.

"Baby, don't trip. Everything's going to be cool," Sin said. Alonzo ran to the bedroom and came back out with Shaunté's jewelry.

Sin smiled. "You niggas better hope I don't *never* find out who ya'll is. Niggas wanna hide behind them masks and shit," Sin sneered.

"You keep talking I'm going to take the mask off," Alonzo said. Sin knew if Alonzo took the mask off then he and

Shaunté would be killed because they saw his face. Sin just kept looking at him.

"Let's be up and out," Jeff said as he picked up the money. Alonzo followed him to their car and they left.

"I recognized one of them nigga's voices. You got some scissors?" Sin asked. Shaunté was shaking badly.

"They in the top drawer in the desk," she said. Sin stood up and went to her desk and got the scissors. He went back to Shaunté who was now standing.

"This shit is going to be hard so be still," he said. They got back to back and Sin felt the tiny space in the ties and slid the scissors in and snipped. Shaunté's hands were free and she cut Sin's ties. Sin pulled his phone out and called Rod.

"Hello!"

"Cuzzo, them fools, Jeff and Alonzo, robbed me. Where them niggas live at?" Sin asked.

"They stay in Hilltop Bayview. I'm going to send Ced and a couple of other cats with you."

"You know I do my thing solo. I need a heater though."

"I'm on my way to Roscoe's. Come up there," Rod said and hung up.

"Take me back to the club," Sin said to Shaunté.

"Shit, I'm going with you!" she said as she hurried off to her room.

Sin had a thought and went to Shaunté's room.

"Hey, how much…" Shaunté was standing there in a white lace thong and matching bra. "*Damn!*" he said as he looked at her from head to toe. He felt his dick getting hard.

"Them punk ass niggas fucked off what I had planned for you," she said as she slipped on some loose fitting black Fubu jeans, a black t-shirt, some black Tims, and a black Fubu jacket. She grabbed a brush and brushed her hair down and put a black beanie on. She then reached in her nightstand and pulled out a 9mm Sig.

"How much them fools get you for?" he asked.

"Fifty-thousand!" Shaunté said. Sin just shook his head.

"You getting it like that?" he asked.

"I do a'ight," she said as she grabbed her keys.

She set the alarm as they went out the door. Sin followed her to a green 97 Yukon. They got in and smashed off.

"So what's up for later?" he asked. Shaunté looked at him as she got on the Warren freeway.

"Anything you can handle," she said and smiled.

"Baby, I been gone for like 4. I might hurt you."
"I wouldn't have it any other way."

When they got to Sin's truck, he got in and took off with Shaunté following. Sin's phone rang when he got to the Grand Avenue exit.

"Hello!"

"Sin, you wouldn't believe who just came in here!" Rod said.

"Who?"

"Alonzo and Jeff!"

"Don't do nothing! I'm 2 minutes from there," Sin said and hung up. He made a right on Perkins and parked three blocks down. Shaunté pulled up behind him.

Sin got the tool kit from the back seat of his truck and took Shaunté's plates off. He then got in her truck.

"Them suckas at Roscoe's," he said. Shaunté pulled her 9mm out and cocked it. When they got to Roscoe's, Shaunté double-parked. Sin called Rod. A few minutes later Rod came out with Ced.

"Them fools ordered to go. They ought to be coming out in a minute," Rod said. Ced slid the Mac 10 to Sin along with another clip.

"Ya'll get up outta here," Sin said.

Rod went back in and got his wife, Paula, and they left in the 98 cream colored V-12 600 Benz. Shaunté got out of the truck and stood next to Sin.

"Here they come!" she said. Sin turned his back and put his hands on Shaunté hips and kissed her. When Jeff and Alonzo were five feet out the door, Sin let Shaunté go. She pulled the 9 out and pointed it at them.

"Next time you hoe cake muthafuckas jack somebody, make sure they don't know your voices," Sin said as he put the red beam on Jeff's head.

"Damn all that! Where my fuckin' money at?" Shaunté asked.

Jeff made a quick move and Shaunté shot him. She pulled her beanie down into ski mask mode. She walked up to Jeff as he crawled on the ground. She made eye contact with Alonzo and put one in Jeff's head.

"Nigga, you next. Let us get that loot," Sin said. Shaunté noticed people looking out the window. She let three slugs off through the glass and it shattered.

"Next one of you look out here you catching one!" she said.

Sin stood to the side kinda in the shadows so no one would be able to identify him.

"Ya'll killed my folks! You gotta kill me now. Because I'm going to kill your families," Alonzo said. Shaunté looked like she couldn't believe what she just heard and got mad.

"You think I'm a fuckin joke?" she asked and shot Alonzo in the head.

"What the fuck you doing? How we suppose to get our fuckin money?" Sin yelled. Shaunté took their Rolex watches, their platinum chains, the money in their pockets, and their keys. She stood up and pointed to the bodies as she heard the sirens.

"Shoot the bodies," she said.

"For what? They dead! Come on!" he said. Before Sin figured it out, Shaunté slightly raised her gun toward him.

"Just do it to make me feel better," she said. Sin figured it out at that moment. *She's sharp*, Sin thought. Sin raised the Mac and lit the bodies up. They jumped in the Yukon and Shaunté mashed off. When they got back to the K5, Sin put her plates back on.

"Follow me," she said. He did just that.

When they got to Shaunté's house he parked in visitors' parking.

"I know you think I fucked up, but I didn't. I know where the money's at. The car that followed us here was a black 98 Buick Regal. The same car that was parked across the street from the restaurant," Shaunté said. Sin smiled.

"Baby, I ain't really tripping. All them suckas got me for is 3 gees. They ripped you for the lotto," Sin said as they walked into her house.

Shaunté took her coat off and rolled a blunt.

"You hungry?" she asked as she lit the weed.

"Baby, I've been gone for a minute. Food's the last thing on my mind," he said as he walked over and leaned down and kissed her on her neck.

"You would wanna eat. Because you gon' need all your strength," she said and giggled.

"Oh, you got it like that, huh?"

"I ain't had no dick in 3 months. I'm fixing to wear your ass out. Go get in the shower, I'll be in there in a minute," she said.

Sin hit the weed and passed it back and went to the master bathroom. He turned the shower on and looked in the mirror. *Damn, I ain't been home 6 hours and I'm already caught up in some murder shit, and this girl don't give a fuck about shooting. I play this one out right, me and little mama could lock some shit up.* Sin took his clothes off and got in the shower.

After Shaunté put the chicken in the oven she went in the bedroom and took her clothes off. Her mobile rang.

"Hello!"

"Tay, the police didn't even stop over here. They parked at both corners for like an hour then left," Déja said.

"Shit, that's cool. Giiirlll, wait till I tell you what happened to *me!*"

"Hold up. We got a problem. When me and Boogie went in that yard, ol' boy wasn't there."

"What the fuck you mean he wasn't there?"

"He was gone. So was his car."

Fuck! "I watched that fool go down!"

"Me too," Déja sighed.

"Get a hold of Lisa and ya'll meet me at the breakfast spot in the morning," Shaunté said and hung up. *If that nigga lived he's going to be trying to get me. I gotta get him first! Fuck it, I'll worry about that tomorrow.*

Shaunté stepped in the bathroom and saw Sin's silhouette through the stained glass shower door. She opened the door and looked down at Sin's dick.

"Oh yeah, it's on for real!" she said as she stepped in.

Sin saw Shaunté's naked body and got super hard.

"It's going down," he said. He turned Shaunté so she was facing the wall. She bent over and grabbed her ankles giving him a view of nothing but pussy. When he got in he tripped on how tight it was.

"Don't cum in me, pull out. I ain't trying to be no baby mama, Sin," she said. Sin fucked her like a champ. *Oh yeah, he might be the one,* she thought.

"Ooooh, harder, Daddy, fuck me harder!" she screamed.

Sin serviced her for like 15 minutes then felt his nut coming and tried to pull out. Shaunté was about to cum too and wouldn't let him. When Sin started coming it felt like Shaunté's pussy muscles tightened.

"Oh *shit!" he said.* Shaunté turned around and kissed him.

"Man, where you been all my life?" she asked.

"Fuck where I been. It's about where I'm at and what we gon' do with this," he said.

"What about your chick? And don't say you ain't got one," she said.

"That bitch we saw at the club was my ex. When I went to jail she went south on me with my loot. Ain't shit happening there," he said as he nibbled on Shaunté ear.

I'm hella feeling this nigga, she thought.

"I like you, baby, but I don't know you. We can take it slow and see where it leads to," she said. They washed up and got out and put lotion on each other.

Shaunté walked into the kitchen butt naked and got the chicken out the oven. When she came back in the bedroom, Sin was rock hard again. He took the food from her and lay her down and crawled between her legs. He raised her legs so that her knees were almost touching her ears. He slid in her and serviced her slow. They went at it for like 45 minutes. Shaunté knew she was in love when it was over and she watched Sin sleeping.

Chapter Three

The Paper Route

Two months later, Sin and Shaunté were going strong. One was rarely seen without the other. The police got Jeff and Alonzo's car and found the money. Eyewitnesses at Roscoe's claimed that the person that murdered them was a female. They weren't able to identify her though.

Rod gave Sin a kilo to come up on. Sin turned that one key into two and gave Rod the $15,500 he owed him. He and Shaunté then turned the $20,000 they made into $30,000 and bought two keys of their own. They had Tay's girls and Sin's 16-year-old homie, Terell, working for them. They had a spot in North Oakland off of 48th and Shattuck, and two spots in East Oakland, one on 29th Ave between East 14th and East 15th Streets and the Bromly spot off Seminary. Every one of their spots averaged at least $7,500 a day.

Shaunté was deeply in love with Sin, and he was in love with her. They were sitting in the Yukon on 46th Street waiting for Rod when the phone rang.

"Hello!" Sin answered as he looked over at Shaunté's thighs. She was wearing a short white Nike tennis dress.

"Sin, why don't you go pick the kids up when they get out of school. You haven't spent much time with them since you been home," Tracy said.

"Tracy, I can't today. I'm flying to Seattle at 6. I'll be back Monday and we'll do something," Sin said as he rubbed between Shaunté's soft thighs.

"Whatever!" she said angrily and hung up. Sin got mad and tossed the phone on the dashboard.

"What she want you to do?" Shaunté asked.

"She wants me to pick the kids up since I ain't really kicked it with them since I been home. Man, muthafuckas don't understand I'm trying to get this shit right so it'll be cool for everybody."

"Baby, we can just change our flight to tomorrow morning. The money ain't going nowhere," she said.

"Where would I be without you?" he asked as he kissed her.

"Wherever you wanna be. Sin, you don't need me, I know this. I need you though. You the one I've been waiting for my whole life. I have *never* felt this way about anyone in my life," Shaunté said seriously.

"Baby, you got it fucked up. I would still be getting money, but I doubt I would be happy. I would probably be with a no good ass, gold digging bitch, like Yvette. I do need you. Baby, you made this shit happen. I'm in love with *you*. You get down like I do. Plus, I'm scared you'd kill me if I cheated on you," he said and laughed.

"Nigga, you better be," she said and leaned over and kissed him.

Just then Rod and Ced pulled up in Rod's '95 SS Impala. The car was five times black with tinted windows, a sun roof, black leather and wood grain interior, and sitting on 20" gold Dayton's. Rod jumped out and got in the Yukon.

"Cuzzo, this 4 birds. Just give me $28,000 now, and 28 when you get back," he said. Shaunté opened her coach bag and took $4,000 out and gave Rod the rest.

"I'm going to Cancun for a week and I need you to handle my business for me while I'm gone," Rod said.

"Well be back Monday morning," Sin said.

"Rod, when you gonna let my baby cop that SS?" Shaunté asked.

"I'll let ya'll get it for 10. Put 5 on it and owe me 5. If you want the rims too I need 12," he said.

Shaunté handed him the $4,000.

"We'll give you some more when we get back," Sin said.

"I'm gone," Rod said and got out. He got back in the SS and pulled off fast.

When they got back to Skyline, Sin called Tracy and told her to pick the kids up and drop them off at his mom's. Shaunté took one key out the duffle bag and put the rest up.

"I'm going to Bromly to take Lisa and Déja some work. Then I'm going to the grocery store. What you want for dinner?" she asked.

"You!" he said.

"You had me for breakfast this morning, and dinner last night," Tay said and kissed him.

"Can a nigga get a little head tonight?" he asked.

"Don't you get some *every* night?" she asked as she stroked his dick through the shorts he was wearing.

"What about a little tester?" he asked as he raised the back of her skirt and rubbed her thonged ass. Shaunté went to her knees and unzipped Sin's shorts and pulled his dick out and started sucking it. Shaunté gave Sin the best head he had had in a long time. He put his hands behind her head and pumped in and out of her mouth.

"Damn, Baby!" he moaned. Shaunté kept at it. Sin felt his nut coming and stopped her. He was ready to fuck. He just couldn't get enough of Shaunté. He pushed her back and pulled his shorts down. He then pulled her yellow thong off. Sin got between Shaunté soft silky thighs and she guided him into her tight wet pussy and he went to work. Shaunté wrapped her legs around him and fucked him back. When they were done she kissed him.

"I love you!" she said.

"I love you too!" They went to the bathroom. Sin washed up and Shaunté turned the shower on and got naked.

"I'll see you when I get back. Make whatever you want for dinner," he said.

"Baby, take the Lexus. I'm buying hella groceries and I'm going to need the truck," she said as she kissed him. He popped her on her naked ass and went to the living room. He picked up his keys and gun and left. He put the E-40 CD in the deck and pulled off.

When Sin got down the hill on 35th and MacArthur he saw Yvette getting into his Camaro in the Taco Bell parking lot. He pulled in and blocked her in. She saw Sin and got scared.

"You think I'm playing, don't you?" he said as he looked in the back and saw the Louis Vuitton suitcases.

"Do whatever you gonna do. I'm tried of all you niggas!" she said.

"Man, fuck you! If your ass wasn't scandalous we wouldn't be going through this shit. Bread me out and we ain't gotta talk again," he said. Yvette looked up at him sadly.

"Get in so I can talk to you," she said. Sin felt like slapping her as he walked around the car and got in.

"You didn't have to burn the Benz up. I would've gave it back to you," she said.

"You lucky I didn't do it while you was in it!" he said.

"I see you doing good for yourself. You pushing a new Lexus, wearing a platinum chain and a Rolex."

"What you thought, the hustle stopped or something? One monkey don't stop no show." Yvette just stared at him. She knew she was wrong for doing him like she did. *I married this cheating ass muthafucka and he got another bitch pregnant. I should've waited for Sin. Now he hates me. I should tell him about Maira.*

Sin had turned Yvette into somebody. When they met they were both 22. Yvette didn't have anything. No car, no job, and she lived with her mama. She was basically a fine, sexy, hood rat. Sin fell for her on sight. He turned her into a woman.

He took her everywhere and bought her everything. He brought out the best in Yvette, and paid for her to go to school so she could have that career she now had in the computer field. He had truly loved her and she paid him back by ripping him off and giving his money to another nigga to come up on. The joke was on her in a real way, because she lost Sin and she still loved him.

"I'm so *stupid.* I lost the only man I ever loved," she said and rubbed Sin's hand. He snatched his hand back. He wanted to knock the bitch out.

"Look man! Before you can even *think* there could possibly be *anything* between us again you gots to make my money right," he said angrily.

"What if I can get us $80,000?"

"I'm listening," he said. Yvette ran her plan down to him.

"If we make it happen, will you take me back?" she asked.

Bitch, is you crazy, Sin thought. "Yeah, for sure," he lied.

Shaunté was passing Taco Bell when she saw her Lexus blocking a candy purple convertible Camaro and Sin talking to a girl she knew from somewhere. She slowed down to try to get over so she could turn into the parking lot. The traffic was too thick so she had to go up two blocks and make a U-turn. Then it hit her who the chick was. *Oh no this nigga ain't!* She punched the gas, and when she got back they were gone. Shaunté started crying as she pulled out and went to the freeway.

"Your ass wanna play games? We'll play them then!" she said.

Sin picked the kids up and took them to the mall, bought them some clothes and then went home. When he pulled up the Yukon wasn't there. He went in and called Shaunté's cell phone. The voice mail came on so he hung up. At 7:00 she still wasn't home. He called the spot and Terell said he hadn't seen her since she dropped the yayo (cocaine) off. Sin called Déja's house.

"Hello!" she answered.

"Déja, my wife over there?" he asked.

"She was over here around 3:30. She hot at you. She saw you with your ex."

"Fuck! It ain't even what she think. If you talk to her tell her to call my mobile," he said.

"You better hope you catch her before she catches up with her ex." Sin hung up and called Shaunté again.

When the voice mail came on he took a deep breath.

"Tay, it's not even like that. I got something up. I love you, Boo. Call me!" he said and hung up.

●●●●●●

Shaunté hung her phone up and wiped her eyes. Déja shook her head.

"Girl, you got it bad! Why don't you talk to him," she said.

"He got me straight tripping. I'm giving this nigga my all,

Déja. How he gonna do me like that? I ain't went bad on him one time, and niggas be trying to throw dick at me 24-7!"

"Did you see them kissing or something? I mean shit, you did say that hoe peeled him for some loot. Maybe he was trying to get it back," Déja said.

"I'm staying the night over here," Shaunté said.

●●●●●●

At 8:30, Sin was dressed in black cargo sweats, a black T-shirt, black Nike Air Max, and a black leather bomber. He put the 9mm in his coat pocket and picked up his ski mask. The doorbell rang and Sin answered. He paid the pizza man the $25 for two fully loaded pizzas then took them to the dining room.

"Princess, the pizza is here. I gotta go somewhere. I'll be back in an hour. Watch your brother, and you two keep your butts out of me and Tay's room. And if Tay comes tell her I said to call my mobile phone."

"Yes, Daddy," Quesha said and got up and followed him to the door.

"Hurry up and come back, girl, so I can beat you down in Madden Football!" Malik said.

"Boy, you can't beat me!" Quesha said as she pulled Sin down and kissed his cheek. When Sin got outside he heard the door lock. He went and got in the Lexus and smashed off.

When Sin pulled up at the little house off of Park Blvd., he saw the Camaro.

He also saw the garage was open just as Yvette said it would be. In there was a gold '87 SS Monte Carlo. He parked the Lexus across the street and got out. He walked to the open garage door and pulled his mask out and put it on. He took the safety off the 9 and went through the door leading into the house.

Yvette said that he was supposed to turn right and come straight down the hall. When Sin got down the hall he saw a short dark skinned dude in a pair of boxers lying on a blue leather couch watching TV. Yvette was sitting in front of a computer in a sheer pale blue robe. She had on her glasses and looked seriously sexy. As Sin stepped into the living room the dude saw him and got up.

"Nigga, don't make me pop you and your broad!" Sin said. Yvette stood up looking scared and the front of her robe opened showing the lavender Victoria's Secret lace panties and bra. Sin had to admit that her body was still banging. The imprint of her pussy in the panties was fat, her long sexy legs were cool, and her big titties were spilling over the top of her bra.

"Lil' mama, tie that nigga hands up," Sin said as he tossed her the wire ties. "He get loose, I'm popping you first!" he said as he looked at the picture of the baby on the mantle. This kid wasn't homeboy's, but it was Yvette's. Sin laughed to himself. Yvette had suckered this fool into taking care of the next nigga's kid. He pointed the gun at her.

"Where the money at?" he asked. Yvette started crying.

"I'll go get it. Just don't hurt me and my little girl!" she cried. *This bitch should've been an actress.* She started going towards the bedroom and Sin stopped her.

"You try anything I'm killing ya'll," he said as she

walked to the back.

"Potna, this ain't nothing personal. You and your broad peeled my nigga, Sin, for his loot. That nigga told me if I was able to get it I could have it."

"Man, she got that nigga. I didn't have nothing to do with it!" he said angrily.

When Yvette came back to the living room she was carrying a gray duffle bag. Sin took the bag and opened it. He shuffled through the stacks of money trying to make sure the stacks were all money and not stacks of paper underneath real bills. When he was satisfied he zipped it up.

"Lil' mama, walk me to the door. I wouldn't want you to try to shoot me in the back," he said. He looked at the dude and shook his head. For a brief second he thought about exposing Yvette, but he got what he came for.

He led Yvette to the garage. He wanted to fuck her badly when he saw how her ass was swallowing the thong she was wearing.

"Turn around," he said. She did and he bent her over the front of the SS Monte Carlo and pulled her panties down. While still holding the back of her neck down he pulled his sweats and boxers down. Yvette reached under her and grabbed his dick and pulled him into her. Sin started fucking her hard.

"Oh, Daddy, I missed you so much!" she moaned.

That made Sin think. Although she had some bomb ass pussy, he really hated her for fucking over him. He pulled out.

"Lick your juice off me!" he commanded. Yvette was only too happy to oblige. She went to her knees and started sucking him up like a pro. He pushed her away and pulled his sweats up.

"Didn't I tell you robbing his ass was going to be easy?" she asked as she stood up pulling her panties up.

This nothing ass bitch! "Not as easy as it was to get your stupid ass for my 50 gees and whatever extras that's in the bag," Sin said as he left out the garage laughing while Yvette stood there looking stupid.

When Sin got home, Tay still wasn't there. He stayed up until 12:30 A.M. then went to their room. When Shaunté came in the next morning she found Sin asleep. She went to the closet and put the money she collected up. When she came out the closet she saw Sin's eyes open.

"Come here, baby," he said softly. She came over to the bed and he slapped the shit outta her.

"Punk ass bitch! This how you carrying it?" he yelled as he slapped her again. "I'm fixing to kick yo' muthafuckin ass!" he added.

"Nigga, this how you wanna act? I caught your punk ass with *that* bitch!" she yelled as she pulled back and slapped him back with all her might. Sin got up and slapped her so hard she saw stars. He was about to hurt her but stopped himself.

"Bitch, this what I did!" he said as he pushed the speaker button on the phone and dialed his voice mail. The message that came on was a pissed off female:

"Sin, you muthafucka! I want my part of the money! You think I went bad when you went to jail? Don't pay me and see what happens!" the voice said and slammed the phone down.

"I let that bitch set up a lick on her dude thinking if I got my money I'd give her the extras and take her hoe ass back! It wasn't about no pussy with me! It was about my fuckin money!" he said as he went to the closet and got the duffle bag and dumped it on the bed.

"That's 96 gees! I did that shit for us!" Sin yelled. He was hella mad. He had to get out of there before he hurt Tay real bad. He walked out the room and Quesha and Malik were in the hallway. Quesha had a scared look on her face. Sin had forgot that she hated violence. When he and Tracy used to get into it Quesha would start crying loudly.

"It's okay, baby. Get dressed. We going to eat," he said as he kissed Quesha on the cheek. He turned and went back in the room. He looked at Shaunté, crazy. He went in the bathroom and jumped in the shower.

When Sin got out he wrapped a towel around him and went into the bedroom.

"Sin, I wasn't with no dude last night. I stayed the night at Déja's house. I was there when you called." He knew where she was because Terell went past there.

"Whatever, man," he said as he called Rod.

"Hello!" Rod answered

"Cuzzo, I got that 28 and the 8 for the car."

"I'll be by your spot in a minute," he said.

"Don't bring that fool, Ced. I don't want niggas knowing where I lay my head. Plus, I don't trust that fool," he said seriously.

"A'ight, I'll be there," Rod said and hung up.

Sin took the towel off and lotioned down. He put on some blue silk DKNY boxers. The only boxers Shaunté wanted him in were silk ones, of which she bought him 30 pairs at a time. Sin didn't care one way or another as long as they were clean.

Quesha came in the room wearing a dark blue Guess jean outfit, an orange Nike T-shirt, and some blue and orange Nike Air Max shoes.

"Tay, will you do my hair?" she asked.

"For sure. Anything for my girl," she said and kissed her forehead. Malik came running in the room wearing some light blue Old Navy jeans, a white Old Navy T-shirt, and some light blue and white Jordan's.

"Where mine?" he asked. Shaunté picked him up and gave him a big kiss on the lips.

"Boy, when you get grown you gonna be my man?" she asked. Malik started grinning.

"And you know this, maaaaann," he said imitating Chris Tucker's Smokey character from *Friday*.

"Fool, you better back up off my chick!" Sin said.

"Aww, Dad, quit hating on a playa," he said. Sin started laughing.

Shaunté put Quesha's hair in Pocahontas braids and she put Malik's hair in six braids that came to his shoulders.

Sin put on some light blue Polo jeans, a dark blue Polo T-shirt, and some black Timberland's. He grabbed the 24" link chain with the cross, a gold wedding band, a 3 carat diamond in each ear, and the Rolex, all of which Shaunté copped him, except for the Rolex that they got off of Jeff. He looked at Shaunté sitting on the end of the bed looking sad.

"Pack our stuff for the flight and get ready to go," he said. Tay's face lit up with a smile. She packed their stuff in two suitcases and then went and got in the shower.

When Tay got out the shower and came back in the room she was naked. Sin walked up and kissed the tattoo of a black panther on her shoulder. He picked the lotion up and squirted it on her body and rubbed it in.

"You fixing to make us late," she moaned. Sin stuck his finger in her and she was major wet.

Shaunté moved away from him and picked up the bottle of Gabbana and sprayed some behind her knees, between her titties, on her wrist, and between her thighs. She put on a blue silk thong, matching bra, and burgundy and black plaid school girls skirt. She grabbed the short sleeved white Guess button up and put it on. She then put on the black Guess sandals. She combed her silky hair down.

Shaunté opened her jewelry box and slid on her 3 carat diamond earrings, her wedding band, a nugget and diamond ring on her right hand ring finger, a small rope with a diamond heart, a small rope bracelet, and her Rolex. They went in the bathroom and brushed their teeth.

"Baby, I'm sorry I pissed you off, but I'm glad ya'll were gone before I came back. I was fixing to be shooting on sight," Tay said. She put her arms around Sin's neck and kissed him.

When Rod came they left. They dropped the SS off at the paint shop then dropped Rod off and took the kids to eat. After they dropped the kids off at home they rode to the San Francisco airport. They parked, and Shaunté climbed over the seat and made her change.

When they emerged from the Yukon, Tay had on a maternity dress and looked like a woman seven months pregnant. Under the dress, she had on a back brace and a rubber padded suit that held 4 kilos in it. She also had on flat shoes and her hair was in a ponytail. Sin smiled at his generosity. As they were getting close to the security gate, Sin had a feeling something wasn't right. He looked around and saw six people who looked like undercover cops.

"Let's go! This shit ain't co…"

A man came out of a side room with a dog. The dude standing behind Sin made a sudden move and Sin was about the fire on him. The dude started running for the exit and one of the females Sin felt was the police grabbed the dude's bag. Sin pushed Tay through the gate. 5 pounds of weed fell on the floor and about ten cops swarmed the dude. Sin sighed. He turned to see Tay on the other side laughing.

When they got to Seattle, Shaunté rented a Nissan Altima. They then went to Sin's cousin Jay's house. Sin used his key to get in. Jay, his girl, Aimee, and their daughter Jaimee were watching TV.

"Why didn't you tell me you were coming today?" Jay asked.

"Nigga, you know that I don't like nobody knowin' when I'm hittin' the highway" he said as he picked Jaimee up and kissed her. He put her down and went to the room they stayed in when they were in town. Shaunté took the maternity dress and padding off and stood there in nothing but her underwear. Sin looked at her. Last night was the first night they didn't have sex. He hit that every night, even on periods.

"You know what, baby?" she asked.

"What, Boo?"

"I love your punk ass," she said playfully.

"Bitch, then why was you sucking on the next nigga dick last night?" he asked.

"I told you where I was at. I would never fuck around on you, no matter what you did," she said seriously.

Sin looked at her tattoos. The one on her left tittie was a red heart with a banner that said "Sin for life". The one on her right tittie said "Down Ass Bitch". Sin's face was tattooed on her left shoulder, and on her right ankle it said "Ride or Die". Sin was gonna have some fun with her.

"I fucked Yvette last night," he said. Shaunté looked at him sadly and shook her head.

"I hope it was worth your life. Because when we get home, I'm gon' kill you and that punk ass bitch!" she said.

Shaunté saw that Sin was laughing and knew he was lying. She started laughing too and wrestled him down on the bed.

"You better stop playing with me like that," she said as she pinned him down with her knees on his shoulders and her pussy in his face. He kissed her thighs.

"We can play later. Get dressed," he said. Tay put the schoolgirl outfit back on.

"Baby, we only have sales for 3 keys. Why you bring the extra one?" she asked.

"These cats out here paying $1,500 an ounce. We gon' drop them for a gee. That will make us $36,000 back," he said.

When they got to the den, Jimmy handed Sin a bag containing $20,000.

"Sin, I know you don't like popping open your packages, but I need a half key too," Jimmy said.

"Bring me two of them and call Juanda," Sin said to Tay.

Shaunté went in the room and got the dope and brought it back. Jimmy set the triple beam scale up and gave Sin two zip lock freezer bags. Sin weighed out 18 ounces and bagged it and gave it to him. Jimmy handed him another $10,000. Shaunté pulled her phone out and dialed a number.

"Hello!" the female voice answered.

“What’s up, bitch?” Shaunté asked.

“What’s up, hoe? Ya’ll out here?”

“Yeah, we’ll be over there in a minute.”

“You taking care of my man?”

“You know it”

“You better be. Because I swear you *don’t*, I’m gon’ let him *stand up* in my pussy,” Juanda said.

“Keep dreaming, bitch. I puts it on him. He ain’t going nowhere.”

“I’ll see ya’ll when you get here,” Juanda said and hung up.

Sin liked Juanda and Shuanda. They were twin ex-strippers and he wanted to have a session with either one of them. If Shaunté fucked up, he would be on the first thing smoking to Seattle. He knew he could fuck either one of them by the way they flirted with him. Shaunté went and put the money up and grabbed another key and they left.

When they pulled up on Lincoln Street they stopped in front of a nice peach stucco house. There was a black Expedition parked in the driveway. They got out and walked up the walkway. Juanda opened the door and pulled Sin in and shut it before Tay could come in.

“Don’t make me shoot this joint up over my man,” Tay said laughing.

"What's up, Daddy? You need to push her to the left and come see what a real woman feels like," Juanda said as she kissed him and gently bit his lip.

"You playing," he said. Juanda grabbed his dick and licked her lips. Juanda was top notch for real. She was Indian and Black, had long naturally curly black hair, honey colored skin, a beautiful face, and a helluva body. She stood at 5'9" and weighed 135 pounds. She had big sexy thighs, a small waist, wide hips, 36C titties, and a big, sexy bouncy ass. Sin got hard in her hands.

"We'll see what we can put together," he said as he pinched her hard nipple through her wife beater and went to the kitchen.

Juanda opened the door. Shaunté playfully pushed her. They came in the kitchen and Shaunté opened the back pack and pulled the kilo out and handed it to her. Juanda left the room. Sin loved the way her braless titties and ass bounced in the white wife beater and unbuttoned short-shorts. She came back and handed Shaunté the money as the phone rang. She went to answer it and Sin's eyes was glued to her ass. Shaunté noticed this.

"You wanna fuck her?" she asked.

"Baby, I told you if I fucked another chick you would be fucking her too," he said seriously.

"I'd let her eat my pussy," Shaunté said.

"Would you eat hers?" she asked.

"I would have to be in that type of position to answer that."

They heard the front door open and close. Shuanda, Juanda's twin sister, walked in wearing some white Nike leggings, a red Nike sports bra, a white Nike wind breaker, and some red and white Air Max. They could see through the pants that she had on red panties.

"Oh, here comes the other Indian hoe," Shaunté said as she and Shuanda hugged. For some reason Sin like Shuanda a little more. Shuanda sat on Sin's lap and put her arms around his neck.

"So when you gonna dump this broad and get with me? I got it good. On my knees or on my back. She probably don't even suck it good," Shuanda said.

"Bitch, I be having this nigga out his body when I suck his dick," Shaunté bragged. "But now, I'll let him test out your head if he wants to," she added playfully.

Shuanda had Sin's dick super hard. He made it jump and she looked at him and giggled. She looked back at Shaunté.

"If I suck his dick he ain't never coming back to your ass."

"We'll see ya'll in two weeks," he said as Shuanda got off of him and went to the counter. *Damn! Her ass is wearing a thong.*

Sin and Shaunté went and saw another dude they knew from Oakland and served him the last key. When they were done they went back to Jay's house. Shaunté kicked it with Aimee and Jaimee. Sin left with Jay. Jay had a cool amount of clientele. Some cats came through looking at Sin crazy. He started laughing. *These dudes just like niggas everywhere else!*

Chapter Four

Keep it Movin'

When Sin and Shaunté got back to Oakland, they put down a serious grind, leaving their house at 11 every morning and not coming back home until 3 the next morning. The money was looking so cool sometimes Sin just stayed on the block until 6 a.m. selling rocks. This routine had Sin tired. When Friday came he was looking forward to kicking back for the weekend. Rod was leaving that night for Cancun and was leaving Sin with 20 keys. Sin only had to give him back $250,000. That was less than 13 a key. The regular price in the street was 17-5. That would bring Sin $100,000 for himself.

Sin was at the light on Havenscourt and Bancroft on his way to Sherry's Final Stop to get his hair cut, when he saw Quesha's mom, Kesha. He hadn't seen her since he'd been home from prison. He just shook his head. The dope was tearing her down. He started thinking about how she was when they met.

Sin was 18 and Kesha was 16 and she was a knockout. She was light skinned, had short styled hair, dark brown eyes, and a beautiful face. She stood at 5'11", and weighed 140 pounds. She had long sexy legs, wide hips, a medium waist, 36DD titties, an almost flat stomach, and a big round ass. Sin had to have her.

Kesha was about to get into a fight with some of the chicks that hung out on the block. Sin was just coming out the store when he heard the arguing.

"Baby Girl, you way too cute to be out here scrapping," he said to her. Kesha looked at Sin.

"These ugly jealous ass bitches ain't fixing to be out here talking shit to me!" she said.

"Tiff, ya'll get up outta here with that punk ass shit," he said. The four girls walked away mad. Sin got Kesha pregnant a month later. They broke up when Quesha was 2 years old. Sin had bitter feeling towards Kesha after that.

Sin first found out Kesha was on dope was when he picked his daughter up from school one day. When he walked into the class and saw his 4 year old daughter sitting there, hair wild, clothes wrinkled, and face dirty, he got pissed. The pre-school teacher, Mrs. Wright, told him that this had been going on for over a month and if things didn't change she was going to call Child Protective Services and have Quesha taken.

Sin took Quesha to his and Tracy's house in Castro Valley, then rode to the apartments on 98th Ave. where Kesha lived. He got out of the burgundy wine '92 drop Iroc and went to the door. He stepped back and kicked it off the hinges. There were like eight crack heads inside smoking dope. Sin went smooth off up in there. He put hands on everybody in the house. He threw Kesha's boyfriend, Dale, through the sliding glass door and over the balcony. He then beat Kesha's ass. After he calmed down, which took about a month, he made Kesha sign over custody of Quesha to him.

Sin shook his head and pulled the Lexus over across the street from the shop. He got out and walked down the street towards Kesha. She was looking dirty and beat down. A young dude was walking up to her with a stick in his hand.

"Bitch, what's up with my money?" he yelled.

"I told you I would pay you when I got it," she said as she

saw Sin and the look on his face.

"Ponta, what you fixing to do with that stick?" Sin asked.

"What you in my business for?" the dude asked with an attitude. Sin got within an inch of his face.

"Nigga, fuck the dumb shit. You even *act* like you gon' hit my baby mama with a stick, I'm killing you!" Sin said. The young cat stood his ground and Sin respected that.

"You must be about to pay me what she owe me," he said.

"How much you owe this nigga?"

"Fifteen dollars," Kesha mumbled.

"*What! Fifteen dollars!* Nigga, that's all your life's worth?" Sin asked as he pulled a knot of money out his Girbaud Jeans pocket.

He peeled $20 off and threw it in the dude's face.

"Next time I'm lighting your ass up. Stay away from her," Sin said as he nodded for Kesha to follow him.

"When was the last time you saw Quesha?" he asked as they stopped in front of Sherry's.

"I saw her on her birthday. How long you been out?" she asked.

"About two months. Never mind that though. Kesha, her birthday was *seven* months ago. Man, when you gon' get yo shit together?" he asked.

"Don't fuckin preach to me, Sin. I ain't trying to hear that shit! When you gon' get yours together? You need to worry about that bitch and the next nigga riding around in your shit," she said.

"Man, you know what? Fuck you! Next time I see a nigga about to bust your head I'm letting him," he said as he went in the shop.

While the barber was giving Sin a bald head he noticed the young cat and two other dudes looking through the window. *Damn, I left my strap in the car.* He pulled his phone out and called Tay.

"Hello!" she answered. Sin heard music in the background.

"Baby, where you at?" he asked.

"I'm just leaving the house. I'm on High street and MacArthur," she said.

"Bring a heater up to the barber shop."

"I'll be there in a minute," she said and hung up.

Sin sat back and went deep into thought. *I need to make 500 gees and I'm out this shit. I'll buy me a club and go legit. Put a baby in Tay and get married.*

Sin heard the SS coming a block away. He saw Tay pull up with Lisa, Déja, and Terell. They had got the SS painted light green with a dark green base. The black leather was now green, green tints, wood grained steering wheel and dash and panels. They threw in four 15 inch JL woofers, four 6x9 JVC 4 ways, a

JVC deck with the CD changer in the trunk, a remote, and two 1,000 watt Zeus amps.

Tay got out of the car wearing a white Channel tennis dress, red Channel flip-flops, and a Channel headband over her braids. Lisa was dressed exactly the same, except her dress was red, flip-flops white, and Déja was in yellow and white. Terell was with them. He stopped and talked outside to the young cats. When they came in, the whole shop went silent. Every dude up in there was quiet. Sin gave J, the barber, $20 and then got up and kissed Shaunté. They went to the back where the bathroom was. Shaunté handed Sin the gun.

"Who you trippin' on?" she asked.

"I had to check one of them fools outside for disrespecting Kesha," he said.

"I gotta surprise for you when you get home," she said and kissed him again.

They walked back into the main area, and some ancient nigga with a perm that was sitting up under the dryer stuck his foot out to stop Shaunté. "What's up with you, Boo?" he asked. Shaunté looked at the dude.

"You don't see my man right here?" she asked.

"And? My name's John," he said.

Shaunté looked at Sin and saw him nod his head. The first thing Sin noticed was the diamonds dude had on.

"Nigga, if I *gave* a fuck about this bitch I'd split your wig," Sin said. He figured if the nigga was bad enough to get at his broad in front of his face, he was bad enough to deal with the repercussions, and that was un-assing his riches.

"Nigga, fuck you! Your bread ain't long anyway, ol' broke ass nigga," Shaunté said as she sat next to homeboy.

"Yeah, hoe? Three's good, four's a crowd anyway," Sin said as he put his arms around Déja and Lisa. Shaunté looked at homeboy.

"My name's Sharon, baby. Call me later on," she said as she wrote her number down.

"Bitch, come get your shit out my house!" Sin said. Shaunté stood up and they all walked out.

"Tee, these niggas your folks?" Sin asked Terell as he pulled the Glock 40 out.

"I know them from school. Why, they tripping or something?" Terell asked angrily.

"You need to holla at them before they fuck around and get some hot ones," Sin said.

Kesha saw the gun from across the street and just knew Sin was about to kill the youngster. "Sin, no!" she screamed. Sin gave Terell the Lexus keys.

"Follow us!" he said. He and Shaunté went and got the SS and left.

"Who was that bitch across the street screaming your name?" Tay asked.

"That's Quesha's mom, Kesha," he said. Shaunté turned her lip up and frowned.

"Uhh, you was fucking that?" she asked.

"Shut the fuck up! Your ass always got some stupid shit to say!"

"Nigga, you shut up!" she said. Sin jerked the wheel to the right and slammed on his brakes and skidded next to the curb.

"Get the fuck out!" he yelled as he hit the lock button. Terell pulled up behind them and Shaunté got out.

"Man, you tri..." Sin burned rubber before Shaunté finished her sentence. He pulled his phone out and made two phone calls then went and picked the kids up from school. He kicked it with them for little while then made a 5 key and 1 key sale.

Sin pulled up in a short-term parking lot at the Oakland International Airport at 5:30. He got out the K5 and slid his gun in the console and grabbed his backpack. He went to the ticket counter and gave the lady $300for the round trip ticket. He went and boarded the plane and pulled his CD player out and put the C-Bo CD in and knocked.

••••••

When Sin got to Seattle he grabbed his bag and got off the plane. He walked through the airport and went and stood outside the terminal. *"Beep Beep!"* He turned and saw Shuanda's black Expedition and walked toward it. When he opened the door Juanda was sitting there. She was wearing a short, Dolce Gabana skirt and a white belly T-shirt. Sin got in and closed the door.

"Come on, I'm leaving at 6:30," he said.

"Baby, I got something cool planned for your ass," she said as she pulled off.

"What you got on up under there?" he asked as he touched her thigh.

"Nothing. I don't wear panties," she said. Sin turned on the dome light and lifted the front of her skirt and saw a fat shaved pussy.

"Oh yeah, it's going down!" Sin said.

"No baby, I'm going down," she said and gave Sin a seductive smile.

"Don't let it slip out that I was out here. Shaunté will kill us both," he said.

●●●●●●

Shaunté was sitting at home in some sexy lingerie waiting for Sin. She cooked, bought some scented candles, and put a bag of rose petals in the tub and on the bed. She had called him twice and he hadn't answered his phone. She called again and the voice mail came on.

"Look Daddy. I'm sorry I made you mad. Come home, please. I love you!" she said and hung up.

Chapter Five

It's Gong Down Tonight

When Sin and Juanda pulled up in front of her house he was having second thoughts. They got out of the truck and he thought about what he was doing and smiled. He was about to get down with one of the finest chicks he had ever seen in his life. When they walked in, Shuanda was sitting on the white leather sofa in a short sheer white baby doll nightie, smoking a blunt. Sin could see her big titties and brown nipples clearly.

"Hey, honey!" she greeted.

"What's up?" he asked as he sat next to her.

"You wanna hit this?"

Sin gave her a sexy smile. "Fa sho!" he said as he licked his lips suggestively. Shuanda started laughing.

"Nigga, I was talking about the weed, but you never know," she said. Sin noticed how her nipples started poking through the nightie.

"I'll be back," Juanda said and walked toward her room.

"So your wife pissed you off, huh?" Shuanda asked.

"Something like that," he said as he passed her the weed back.

"You guys come in here," Juanda said.

Sin followed Shuanda into the bedroom. Juanda had on

the same style nightie her sister had on but hers was red. Sin kicked his shoes off and he and Shuanda got on the bed and they all smoked.

"You want a massage?" Shuanda asked.

"For sure," he said.

"Get undressed," Juanda said.

"Y'all undress me," he said. Shuanda took his jacket and shirt off and Juanda took off his pants.

"Lay back, baby," Shuanda said.

"What's up? Can I get my fantasy fulfilled?" Sin asked.

"What's your fantasy?" Juanda asked.

●●●●●●

"You know what Sin? Fuck you! Come and get your stuff. I ain't fucking with you no more!" Shaunté yelled into the phone. She hung up and went to the bedroom to get her cell phone. She took it off the charger and scanned the numbers until she found the one she was looking for. She called and waited as the line rang. After the fourth ring it was picked up.

"Hello!" a male voice answered.

"John, this is Sharon. I met you at the barber shop earlier."

"What's cracking, lil' mama? You know I'm trying to kick it with you tonight," he said.

"Where you wanna meet?" she asked.

"Echelon," he said.

"I'll be there in an hour," she said and hung up.

Shaunté got up and put on a light green Prada dress and the matching open toe Prada heels. The dress was cut low in the front setting her cleavage out nicely. It was short and came thigh-high and sculpted her hips and ass. She grabbed the matching purse out her closet. She took her Glock, her wallet, and a few other things out of her Coach and put it in the Prada bag. As she picked up Sin's green and black Leather Sean John jacket, she thought about the reaction Sin would have. He would no doubt beat her ass.

I'm just going to feel John out to see if he's ripe for the plucking, she said to herself as she picked up her keys and left. She jumped in the Lexus and rode off.

●●●●●●

"My fantasy is to get with both ya'll," Sin said. Shuanda was massaging his back and Juanda was rubbing his legs.

"I don't swing like that, and if I did it wouldn't be with my sister," Shuanda said.

"I do, and I would do it with Shuanda. Shit, she fine as hell. It would be like fucking myself," Juanda said as she gently bit Sin on the ass.

"You are too conceited. And no, it ain't going down like that. He get another girl and I'm sure your ass will hook it up," Shuanda said to her sister.

"Can I get a strip show?" Sin asked. The girls gave him the best strip show he'd ever seen. He loved the way they simulated sex. Juanda's phone rang and she ran in the living room, ass bouncing.

"If it ain't going down like that, then why ya'll both trying to seduce me?"

"We both want to fuck you, baby. We couldn't decide who was gon' get the dick. So we said that we both would. We've shared a nigga before. I *would* rather have some solo time with you," Shuanda said.

Juanda came back in grinning. "I'm going to Bridget's, but before I go, I'm going to do what I've been wanting to do for the last two months," she said.

Juanda pulled Sin's boxers off. She then licked from his balls up to the tip of his dick. She sucked up and down and Sin wanted to laugh. Juanda gave sloppy head, but it felt good, and the way her head bobbed and the sounds she made turned him on. She had nothing on Shaunté though. He looked at Shuanda and stuck his tongue out. She crawled over and straddled his head. As soon as his tongue made contact with the clit Shuanda started riding his head fiercely. For some reason Sin started feeling guilty about cheating on his girl and his dick went soft. He pushed Shuanda off him and moved away from Juanda.

"What's wrong?" Juanda asked.

"I can't do this."
"Why?" she asked.

"He's sprung on his woman," Shuanda said. Juanda frowned at him and shook her head.

"Nigga, do you know how many niggas would kill to be where you're at now?" she asked.

"More like how many done already been where I'm at," he said angrily.

"I'm outta here. It's a bitch sitting at a club right now waiting for me to show up so she can take me somewhere and eat me 'til the sun comes up," she said as she got up and switched to the bathroom.

Sin put on his boxers and Tim's and went to the living room and got his phone. He checked his voice mail and heard all Shaunté's messages. He speed dialed her.

"What?" she answered as soon as she saw Sin's number flash across the caller ID.

"Where you at?" he asked.

"I'm going to meet my date," she said.

"Bitch, don't play with me!" he said through clenched teeth.

"Nigga, I'm serious. You gonna get enough of playing with *me!*"

"Don't do nothing you're going to regret."

"I'm not going to regret shit," she said.

"So that's how it is?" Sin asked. Shaunté started crying.

"What do you want from me? I love you, I do whatever

you say, and I would die for you! What the hell else can I do, Sin?"

"Bitch, you wanna go on your date, go on. I don't give a fuck! I'm in Seattle with the twins anyway," he said.

'Nigga, quit lying! You and them hoes know what I'll do. You ain't stupid, and neither are they, and I'm 'sho bout that!" she yelled and hung up.

Sin walked back in the house and Shuanda was sitting on the couch naked smoking her weed. He walked over to her and grabbed her legs and pushed her back and opened them wide and started licking. Shuanda started moaning loud. Juanda came out the room and all she had on was a towel, which was wrapped around her head. She switched places with Shuanda and Sin sucked on her pussy. Shuanda pulled him away from her sister and got on her hands and knees. Sin slid up in the pussy and started fucking her slow. She looked over her shoulder and frowned. Sin knew what she wanted. He grabbed her long hair with his right hand and her left hip with his left hand and started fucking her hard.

"Oh yeah, baby! Fuck her harder!" Juanda said as she laid back on the other end of the couch spread eagle caressing her titties and fingering herself.

●●●●●●●

Shaunté pulled up at Echelon and got out of the Lexus and started walking towards the entrance when she saw John sitting on a silver convertible 98 Camaro Z-28. The car had smoked tints and 18 inch gold ones.

She looked to the side and saw Sin's homeboy, Hasahn,

watching her. *Shit, I'm going to get my ass beat for real!* One of Sin's potna's named Tommy walked up to her.

"Tay, where my nigga Sin at? I need to get a half thang (half of kilo)" he said.

"I don't know where he at. Call him. I'm sure he'll call you back. He sure ain't calling me back," she said and walked off. When John saw Shaunté his eyes lit up.

"Damn, you look good!" he said and hugged her. Shaunté gave him one of her smiles. Just then, Hasahn and one of his and Sin's potnas, Ron, walked up. Shaunté knew it was about to be on.

"What's up, Tay?" Hasahn said.

"What's up, Cuzzo?" she asked.

"Bitch, fuck all this punk ass bullshit. Sin know you out here tramping?" Ron yelled.

"Who the fuck your bitch ass talking to? I'll light your muthafuckin ass up, bitch!" Tay yelled as she pulled the gun out of her purse. Ron's eyes got big. He looked at Hasahn.

"Nigga, what the fuck you looking at me for? You outta pocket. You better hope Sin don't serve your stupid ass," Hasahn said.

John got up off the car like he was somebody big. "Both you niggas outta pocket for even coming over here talking for that sucka," he said. Hasahn pulled his 45 out and slapped the shit outta John. He was fixing to dome John but noticed all the people looking.

"Punk ass nigga, I'm going to see your ass again. It's The Made Circle," he said as he slapped him with the gun again. He then looked at Shaunté. "Put that gun up and go home."

"I ain't going nowhere until this sucka apologizes for disrespecting me," she said. Hasalın looked at Ron.

"I'm sorry," Ron said.

"Ol' dick riding ass muthafucka! You need to get your own shit and quit working for other niggas!" Shaunté said as she stuck her gun in her purse and walked off. *Shit! Sin is going to kill me.* When she saw John pulling out she pulled up on the side of him. He rolled his window down.

"What's up? You wanna go to Reno?" he asked.

"For sure. Follow me to my house," she said as she pulled off. She drove to Déja's house in Berkeley where she left her car. She got in the car with John and they hit the freeway.

●●●●●●

Sin pulled out of Shuanda and put a rubber on. He fucked her silly until they both came. Juanda pulled the rubber off of him and started giving him head again. He was over hard in a matter of minutes. She put the rubber on him with her mouth then pushed him back and straddled him. Juanda rode Sin like she had

hydraulics in her ass. They went at it for a half hour. While Shuanda watched Sin could see a little jealousness in her eyes. When it was over he fell between them breathing hard.

"Damn, that was worth the wait!" he said.

"I'm leaving," Juanda said as she went in the bathroom and washed up. Shuanda cuddled up with Sin.

"So what's the chances of me getting some solo time with you? I don't want you to think I'm a hoe or nothing. I'm hella feeling you and I did this for you. The last time I did some shit like this was ten years ago. Shit, the white dude gave us $2,000 a piece. Sin, I've been wanting to mess with you since I met you," she said as she laid her head on his chest.

"We'll see what we can do," he said.

Sin already knew he and Shaunté were a done deal, and Shuanda trying to get on his line was right on time. He kissed the top of her head. After Juanda left they got up and went in the bathroom and got in the shower. Sin fucked her again under the water. They got dressed at 5:30, and Shuanda took him to the airport. They sat in the car and got high for like an hour. Shuanda looked at him with lust in her eyes. Sin shook his head.

"Naw, Boo! Your ass already wore me out," he said. Shuanda looked at the clock and saw it was 6:30, and Sin's flight left at 7.

She moved the armrest and slid over and kissed him and unbuckled his pants. Shuanda started sucking his dick like the world was about to end. After about 10 minutes she reclined his seat and straddled him and started riding him slowly. Sin turned her over laying her on her back and put a rubber on. He served her with slow deep strokes.

"Yeah, big daddy! Oooh, that's how I like it. Make love to me," she moaned.

When Sin was done he threw the rubber out the window

and straightened himself out.

"When can I see you again?" she asked as she started the truck and drove him to the Southwest terminal.

"I'm going to fly back Sunday. We can do *our* thang and get down like we 'spose to," he said as he kissed her.

"Be careful, baby. I'll call you later on," she said. Sin got out of the truck and went in the airport and boarded his flight. He fell asleep instantly. When the flight attendant woke him he was in Oakland. He smiled at her.

"Thank you," he said. He got off the plane and walked out the airport and got in his K5 and went to his mom's. He left the K5 and got in the SS and went home.

When Sin got in the house he saw the meal Shaunté made, the candles, rose petals, and lingerie, but no Shaunté. Their bed hadn't been slept in so that meant she had been out all night. *I'm gon' kill this bitch!* He turned his phone on and checked his messages. Five were for some money. The last two were from Tommy and Ron. Sin got seriously mad. He called Shaunté's cell and her voice mail came on.

"Bitch, I'm beating your muthafuckin ass! Your hoe ass better call me back in the next ten minutes," he said and hung up.

He went in the bathroom and washed up. When he came out he threw on some blue Fubu jean shorts, a white Nike T-shirt with orange writing and swoosh, and some white and blue Air Max with the orange bubble. He put on the link with the gold weed leaf, the small link bracelet, his 2 carat diamond earrings, and the blue Jacob watch. He called back Rod's clientele and told them all where he would be meeting them. He had 5 different sales for a key. He went to Rod's under spot and grabbed the 5 kilos and left.

••••••

Shaunté woke up at 9:30 the next morning and looked to the side and saw John sleeping. She knew she fucked up bad. *Sin's gonna kill me,* she thought. She hadn't let John fuck her, she just rode his head all night. Her phone rang and it was Sin. *Shit!* She didn't answer. She checked the voice mail and heard the message. Shaunté got up quietly and put John's shirt on and went in the bathroom with her phone. Her hand slightly trembled as she dialed the number.

••••••

Sin was on his way to Kragen's Auto Parts on Broadway to meet Rod's boy, Alvin, when his phone rang. He looked at the caller ID and saw Tay's number, He took a deep breath and answered.

"Bitch, where the fuck your trifling ass at?" he yelled.

"Punk, where the fuck was you at last night?" she yelled back.

"A couple of my potnas saw you at Echelon's in some nigga face. Now I'm going to ask you one more time, hoe. *Where the fuck you at*?" he asked calmly. Shaunté got scared. She knew when Sin was calm, he was past mad.

"In Reno," she mumbled.

Sin started laughing. "Have as much fun as you can, because when you get back, I'm stomping your ass," he said.

"Baby, wait! I didn't do nothing. You was acting funny so I went to kick it," she cried. Shaunté wasn't scared of anything, but when Sin got mad she got nervous. She knew when he was mad he wasn't anything nice.

"Bitch, that's on you. You should've made it worth the punishment," he said and hung up.

Sin's head was all fucked up. He was really gone on Shaunté. She was a female version of him. He knew she loved him, and if he wasn't in Seattle fucking with the twins, this shit wouldn't be happening. He wasn't going to totally cut Shaunté out. She got money like he did, but he was going to make her feel his pain ten times worse.

When he pulled up at Kragen's he saw Alvin. He looked around and everything looked alright. He parked and Alvin got out of his rust colored hooptie 77 Grand Prix and got in the Yukon.

"What's up, boy?" he said and gave Sin a pound.

"Same shit," Sin replied. He handed Alvin the brick and Alvin handed him $17,500.

"I'll be at you in a couple of days," Alvin said and got out. Sin put the money in the console, and once Alvin was gone he got out of the Yukon with his backpack.

He walked to the Burger King next door and saw the chick he was suppose to be meeting, Sheree, in the parking lot sitting in her green 98 Grand Cherokee Limited. He walked up to the truck and she smiled as she popped the lock. He got in and she handed him the cash.

"Sin, I'm $500 short. Can I give it to you later on?" she asked. Sheree was 6 foot even, weighed 138 pounds, average 36B titties, long sexy legs, big thighs, a small 23 inch waist, and 36 inch hips. Sin never saw what her ass looked like because she was always in the car when they did business. She was top notch though. She had a very pretty face. Long silky black hair, full lips, latté skin toned, and the darkest green eyes Sin had ever seen.

"Just give me the $500 on the next one," he said as he handed her the last key he had on him.

"So what's up, Sheree? Can I get some of your time later on?" he asked. Sheree was definitely attracted to Sin but she had strict rules.

"I don't think that's a good idea. Don't get me wrong, you look *good*, but I don't mix business and pleasure," she said.

"Baby, you do business with my cousin, not me. I do my own thing. Sheree, you a *dime*, and I wouldn't respect myself if I didn't put my bid in," he said. Sheree smiled at him.

"What you doing later?" she asked.

"Anything you want."

"Lets go to Frisco and have dinner then hit the movies," she suggested.

"What time you want me to pick you up?" she asked.

"Six-thirty should be cool. I live in Richmond in Hilltop Greens. I'll see you later," he said as he got out the truck.

"Sin, you don't have a girl do you? Because, I don't fuck around like that."

"Nah, she dumped me today."

"Why?" she asked.

"I'll tell you about it later," he said as he walked back to where he was parked and got in the Yukon and rode off. Sin took the $87,000 to Rod's under spot and put it up. He then went and picked his money up from Déja, Lisa, and Terell. When all that was done he went home and got all his money, jewelry, and clothes and put it all in the Yukon. He didn't want to be at his mom's. That seemed like going backwards. He considered a hotel, but decided against it.

When he pulled up at his mom's he saw his brother's silver Viper parked in the driveway. He got out and got some of his stuff out. He used his key and went in.

"Hey, baby!" moms said.

"Ma, me and Tay broke up. Can I sta…"

"Nigga, your grown ass ain't fixing to stay up in here!" June said as he got out of his chair. Sin put the stuff he was carrying down.

"Fool, you think we still kids or something? You can't see *me*. I'll punish your ass!" Sin said as he got within an inch of June Bug's face.

"You two ain't about to be in my house carrying on! I will kick both of your asses! Jung Bug, move!" moms said. June moved and Sin went to his room and put his stuff down.

He made three trips, then put the stuff where it went. He walked into the kitchen where his mom was and kissed her on the cheek. He looked at the clock and saw it was 1:30.

"Ma, will you make sure I'm woke by 5:30?" he asked.

"Okay, sweetheart," she said as she continued to cook. Sin went back in his room and called Sheree and told her to make their reservations. When he lay down he couldn't think of anything but Shaunté. *This bitch got me fucked up,* he thought.

●●●●●●

Shaunté was sitting at the Black Jack table feeling bad. *Man, I ain't fixing to lose my Boo like that. I'm wrong for even being out here with this sucka,* she thought as she looked at John. She smiled at the thought of laying him down for his loot. He was non-stop bragging about his money and possessions. He was an idiot, she thought earlier when she pulled his wallet out and copied down his ID information while he was in the shower. She did the same thing with his car registration when he stopped for gas when they were on their way to Reno.

Shit! I fucked up bad! She put her hand on the back of John's neck and rubbed.

"Baby, I'm ready to go home," she pouted.

"That's cool," he said as he stood and helped her off of her stool and walked her to their suite. By 3:30 they were on the freeway heading back to Oakland.

●●●●●●

When Sin got out the shower he lotioned himself down and put on some blue silk boxers. He put on the black Phat Farm jeans, the white Phat Farm T-shirt, and his black suede Timberland boots. The only thing he changed about his jewels was the watch. He put the Rolex on. He sprayed himself with some Issey Miyake and put on the black Phat Farm jacket. He looked in the mirror and nodded his head. He had 45 minutes to be in Richmond. He got in the Yukon and went and bought some weed. He then went and dropped the truck off at Shaunté's and got in his SS and hit the freeway straight to Richmond.

Chapter Six

A New Point

When he pulled up outside the gates of Hilltop Greens, Sin pulled his phone out and called Sheree. She buzzed the gate and he pulled in and drove to the center of the complex and parked in visitors' parking. He got out and followed Sheree's directions to her door. He rang the bell and when Sheree opened the door Sin shook his head.

"Damn!" he said.

"You like?" she asked as she spun around. She was wearing a tight black Dolce & Gabbana baby T-shirt, a short black and burgundy Dolce & Gabbana plaid skirt, and some black and burgundy Gabbana sandals. Sheree had major ass!

"Hell yeah, you lookin' *right*!" he said.

"I'll be ready in a minute," she said as she switched off to her room. Sheree had a seductive walk and Sin could not take his eyes off of her.

He sat down on the plush fuchsia leather sofa. When Sheree came out she had diamonds in her belly button, and ears. She had on a small nugget bracelet, diamond rings on both middle fingers, and a platinum ladies Rolex with a diamond bezel face.

"Can you put this on me?" she asked as she handed him a small platinum chain with a heart-shaped diamond. He stood up behind her and inhaled the Fendi perfume as he fastened the chain on her neck. He kissed her on the cheek.

"Thank you for letting me be seen with a goddess," he said.

"I'm not really feeling the movies. Wc can go rent some videos and come back here after we eat, if you want to," she said softly.

"Yeah, for sure. After dinner I gotta go take care of something real quick. You riding with me?" he asked.

"Yes," she said as she as she proceeded to the door. Sin followed her.

They went out and walked up to the SS.

"This is nice," Sheree said.

"I'm hella tired. You drive," he said as he gave her the keys. They got in and she adjusted the seats to her liking and they pulled off. Sin picked up the remote and pushed the play button, and H-Town's *A Thin Line Between Love and Hate* came on knocking hard.

"I love this song!" Sheree said.

"Yeah, it's cool," he said as he lit the weed and passed it to her.

"So you gonna tell me why you and your girl broke up?" Sheree asked. Sin gave her the watered down version leaving the twins out. Sheree looked pissed.

"That's fucked up that she did you like that," she said.

●●●●●●

When Shaunté got home she found all Sin's stuff gone. She changed clothes and cleaned up, then she called him.

"Hello!" he answered.

"We need to talk, baby," she said.

"Tay, it s too late to talk, you fucked up."

"Sin, I'm not going out like that! I got too much invested in this relationship. I didn't do nothing in Reno but lay the ground work to jack that sucka from the shop. I got his whole script. I did this for us, and if we can't work out our problems, then the time we've been together was for nothing," she said.

"I guess it was then," he replied and hung up.

"Fuck!" Shaunté screamed throwing the phone against the wall.

●●●●●●

After Sin hung up, he and Sheree ate dinner. Bubba Gump's was a nice restaurant and the food was off the hook. The name of the restaurant came from the movie, *Forest Gump.* Sin and Sheree had cool conversation and by the end of dinner they could tell they were really feeling each other. When they were leaving Sin's phone rang.

"Hello!" he answered not recognizing the number.

"Say man, this is Moe. Rod told me to call you," he said.

"What you trying to do?" Sin asked.

"I'm trying to run 3 laps in 17 minutes, each lap," he said.

"Man, you can't do it like that. It's gonna take 17 and a half minutes, each lap," Sin said.

"Alright. Where you gonna make it happen at?" he asked.

"I'm fixing to take my girl to get some ice cream on Seminary and MacArthur in an hour. I'll call you when I get back," Sin said and hung up. *Three keys for $17,500 in an hour!*

Sin gave Sheree directions to the spot.

"So where your dude at?" he asked.

"Sitting in Folsom with life," she said.

"So you down for that cat?" he asked.

"If I was I wouldn't be in the car with you. I'm not the hoe type."

"So you ain't fucking with nobody else?"

"Nope," she said as she pulled up at Sequoia School. Sin got out of the car and ran across the schoolyard and came out the gate across the street from the under spot. He went in and picked up the phone and called the block.

"Hello!" Lisa answered.

"Lisa, ya'll ready?" he asked.

"We only got one zip left (an ounce)," she said.

"A'ight, I'll be there in a minute. Have that loot ready."

"Your wife just pulled up," she said.

"I don't have a wife. I'm happily single," he said and hung up. He pulled out 4 keys and put them in a backpack and left.

When Sin and Sheree got to Baskin Robbin's they went in and got a banana split to share. When they walked back to the car a blue 91 Toyota 4 Runner pulled up. Sin and the dude made eye contact. The dude got out and opened the back of the truck he was in and pulled out a big red toolbox. Sin went to the car and opened it and pushed the button to pop the trunk.

"Man, my woofer in the back keeps going out," Sin said loud enough for all to hear. Moe went and sat in the back seat and pulled the $52,500 out the toolbox. He then took 3 of the 4 keys out the backpack and put them in the box and the money in the backpack.

"Try it now," Moe said.

Sin pointed the remote at the car and pushed the button to change the CD's. The Isley Brother's classic, *In Between the Sheets*, came on. Sin raised the volume to 7 and had the windows on all the shops rattling. He shook Moe's hand then got in the passenger side of the SS. Sheree got in on the driver side and pulled off.

Sin reached over and held Sheree's hand.

"I'm hella diggin' you. I hope we can get to know each other."

"I'm feeling you too. Most niggas getting money like you do are straight assholes, and they hella fake. You ain't nothing like that. You're hella cool, you know, down to earth," she said as she squeezed his hand.

"Baby, money didn't make me. I'm the same nigga I was when I was broke, and I was serious when I told you this was Rod's shit. I'm only copping like 4 keys," he said.

"I ain't star struck or a gold digger anyway. I'd be feeling you even if you worked at McDonald's," she said.

●●●●●●

"Shaunté, you hella stupid! This nigga treated you better than any nigga you ever had and you did some dumb shit like that because he wouldn't call you back?" Lisa asked angrily. Lisa kind of had a crush on Sin and she envied the way he and Shaunté connected. *Why couldn't I have taken my ass to that club that night?* she thought.

"Lisa, I ain't trying to hear that shit right now! I know I fucked up. I'll make it right too," Shaunté said. Just then they heard somebody approaching the block knocking *In Between the Sheets.* They saw the SS pull up across the street from the apartments and Shaunté frowned when she saw Sheree driving. *Don't look like she going to get the chance to make shit right,* Lisa thought.

Sin saw Shaunté standing there in a white, wrap around skirt, a green tank top, and some green sandals. Her hair was in a ponytail and when she turned and looked at them, right there at that moment, he knew he had it bad.

"My ex is over here. We can just have my folks meet us somewhere," he said.

"I ain't tripping. Handle your business," Sheree said as she looked out the window and saw Tay and Lisa. "Which one is she?" she asked.

"The one wearing the green," he said as he got out. He walked across the street where Shaunté and Lisa were. He handed Lisa the brown wrapped brick. She gave him a cookie can containing 9 gees.

He took Shaunté's house and car keys off his ring and handed them to her.

"Let me get my keys," he said.

"Oh, you just going to floss a bitch in my face?"

"I didn't know your ass was over here! Just give me my keys and I'm gone," Sin said angrily.

Shaunté handed Sin the keys. "You must think I'm some type of punk ass bitch or something," she said.

"You lucky I don't beat your ass. You should've thought about that before you went hoeing."

"What you tripping for? You riding around with bitches," Shaunté yelled. Sheree got out of the car.

"Check this out, sweetheart. I ain't about to be too many more bitches. If you was a *real* woman you would be with your man, not me," Sheree said.

"Fuck you, bitch! After he finish beating up your whore out pussy and riding your head, he'll be back, and I'm sure of that!" Shaunté said confidently. Sheree laughed at her.

"Wrong again, bitch. When I do suck his dick and give him some pussy, you all the way ass out, and I'm sure 'bout that!" Sheree said.

"Whatever, bitch!" Shaunté said. Just then Terell pulled up in his 5.0. He looked at Sheree.

"Damn!" he said.

"I got your boyfriend!" Sheree sang.

"Bro, holla at me in the morning," Sin said as he went to the car.

"Sin, your ass bet' not get in that car or you gon' be sorry!" Shaunté said.

"I'm already sorry! I'm sorry that I wasted all this time on your scandalous ass," he said. He looked at Sheree. "Come on, baby" he said. He and Sheree got in the car and Sheree laughed at Tay as she drove off.

"I'm fixing to kill this nigga and that bitch!" Shaunté said as she walked over to the Yukon got in and smashed off following the SS. She grabbed the 9mm out the console and cocked it.

Sin and Sheree stopped at the store on Seminary and MacArthur and went in and got some Remy XO and some Vega's. They came out and headed towards the freeway.

"I'll give you credit. Your ex is cute and has a nice body, but she is a bitch," Sheree said.

Sin looked out the window when Sheree stopped at the

light at the freeway entrance on MacArthur. He saw the Yukon pull up fast and slam on the brakes.

"Go through the light!" he yelled. When he saw Tay's window some down he knew she was going to start busting.

"What?" Sheree asked.

"Go!" he yelled. Sheree punched the gas and an oncoming car almost hit them. She jerked the wheel and made the SS slide to the right missing a car. She got on the freeway going 75. Sin looked out the back window and saw the Yukon coming up on them fast.

"Open this muthafucka up!" he said. Sheree opened the SS up to 110 and they left Tay way behind.

"Damn, talk about fatal attraction! What you do to that girl?" Sheree asked.

"I guess I just got it like that," he said.

"We'll have to see about that!" she said as she reached across the seat and put her hand behind his head and rubbed.

"Girl, that's my sensitive spot. You abut to start something," he said. Sheree kept rubbing. Sin picked up the remote and changed CD's and played some old school Regina Bell. *Baby Come to Me* came on pounding.

When they got to Sheree's she put *The Best Man* in the DVD.

"I'll make us a drink," she said. She went in the kitchen and made their drinks and brought them back then went to her room. Sin rolled a blunt and sipped his drink. When Sheree came back she was wearing a short pink babydoll.

"You look tired," she said.

"I am. I flew to Seattle last night and came back early this morning," he said as he passed her the weed.

"You wanna spend the night? I'd hate for you to fall asleep at the wheel and have an accident," she said. Sin smiled at her.

"Is it cool?" she asked.

"I don't usually let niggas stay the night unless it's my man. Like I said though, I'm really feeling you. You should have the best, and without a doubt that would be me. One thing though. I don't care how much I like you, you ain't hitting it on the first night."

"Baby, I respect that," Sin said.

Sheree got up and took Sin's coat and hung it in the closet. She then came back and sat down on the floor in front of him and took his shoes off and rubbed his feet.

"That feels good," he said as he put the blunt to her lips. She hit it twice as her phone rang. "Hello!" she answered.

"Ree, I need to come get 2 cookies," the female said.

"Jada, hurry up. Me and my dude about to go to bed," she said.

"Your dude? Whaaat! You got a man, Ms. Picky?"

"Jada, just come on," Sheree whined. She hung up and started rubbing Sin's feet again.

"I'm your dude?" he asked.

"You don't wanna be?" she asked. Sheree's mobile rang.

"What!" she yelled as she answered.

"Sheree, this is Von. I need 18 of them thangs," he said.

"V, meet me at the gate in front of my building in ten minutes," she said and hung up.

"Baby, my cousin and potna's on their way. You wanna go up front with me or you wanna kick back?" she asked.

"Take the SS and bring that backpack in," he said. She stood up and went in her room and put on a red hoodie, some white, skintight Capri pants, and some Sheryl Swoopes Nikes. She came back and went out on the balcony and grabbed the dope. She came back in and kissed Sin on the lips and went out.

Sin pulled his phone out his pocket and called Shuanda.

"Hello!" she answered.

"What up, baby?" he asked.

"Nothing. You got me hella sore. You was trying to kill my little stuff."

"Shit, that was you. You was trying to put that thang on me," he said.

"I know, I was, huh. Did it work?" she asked.

"Oh yeah, for sure that," he said.

"Sin, I'm going to ask you a question and this will tell me how much you know about me and how serious you are about us. What's the difference between me and Juanda?" she asked.

"Your eyes are a little lighter than hers, her legs are a little more bowed that yours, you got more ass than she does, and you have a tiny mole on your left tittie," he said.

"You passed the test. That thing we all did ain't going down like that mo more. Oh, and we need to see you on some business."

"I'll call and let you know tomorrow."

"A'ight," she said. Sin hung up and tossed his phone. *Shit, now I gotta teach somebody else the game on getting on the plane.*

When Sheree came in there was a cute petite girl with her. "My cousin wanted to meet you," she said.

"Girl, he is cute. My name's Jada," she said.

"I'm Sin."

"Your car is nice."
"It's just a little something."

"Well, let me get out ya'll's way. Have fun!" she said as she left out the door.

Sheree changed back into the babydoll and came out and locked the front door. She handed Sin his back pack. He dumped the money out and they counted it. They came up with $61,500. Sheree lit the weed as Sin put the money back in the backpack.

"Lay down," she said as she patted her lap. He lay his head in her lap and they smoked the rest of the weed. Sin ended up falling asleep.

"Come to bed, baby," Sheree whispered in his ear. He opened his eyes and looked up at her then he bit himself on the hand.

"Why you do that?" she asked.

"I had to make sure I wasn't dreaming," he said. Sheree leaned down and kissed his lips.

"Did that feel real?" she asked.

"I'm not sure. I think I need another one." She kissed him again, tongue and all. Sin grinned at her.

"Oh yeah, that was real."

They got up and went to the bedroom and Sheree lit two candles on the headboard. She walked up to Sin and took his shirt off of him. She then unzipped Sin's pants and pulled them down and he stepped outta them. They got in the queen-sized bed and Sheree scooted back against him.

"You feel so good," she sighed. Sin moved her hair to the side and kissed her on the neck.

"You do too," he said. They lay there until they both

drifted off to sleep. Sin's last thought was of Shaunté.

Sheree woke Sin up the next morning.

"Baby, your phone's ringing," she said. Sin grabbed the phone from her.

"What?" he asked.

"Say, folks, this Moe. I'm running two miles faster," he said.

"I'm not out that way yet. I'll call you when I get out there," Sin said and hung up. He looked at the time on the phone and saw it was 9:00. Sheree rolled over on top of him and straddled him.

"How did you sleep?" she asked.

"Like a baby," he said as he pulled the nightie over her head and stared at her titties.

Sheree had cool titties. They were a little more than a mouth full. Sin found when a woman was not totally perfect he was more attracted to them, and Sheree's imperfection was her chest. He pulled her down and kissed her. Sheree got up and switched her Jell-O-booty into the bathroom and turned the shower on. She came back out and stood in front of the bed and put her nightie on.

"Take a shower. I'm going to go and cook you something to eat. There's a new toothbrush on the counter," she said as he left the room.

When Sin finished getting dressed he went and ate.

Sheree cooked shrimp and crabmeat omelets, smothered potatoes, waffles with strawberry syrup, orange juice and coffee.

"So, are you going to come over tonight?" She asked.

"If you want me to."

"I wouldn't have asked if I didn't. What you want for dinner?"

"I'm not going to even answer that," he said. Sheree playfully pushed him.

"For real though," she said.

"Cook whatever. I'm not picky," he said a he went to the living room and put his shoes on. Sheree got his coat out the closet and handed it to him.

"Try to be here by 10:00 at the latest. I know how you big ballin' niggas shut shit down at 9."

"I keep shop open all night. I'm tryin to get some proper loot. I'll be here though," he said as he put his coat on.

"Be careful!" Sheree said as she kissed him on the lips. Sin picked up the backpack and his keys and left.

Sin turned his phone back on and checked his messages as he was getting on the 80 freeway going south. He had a sale for 5 keys in Hayward, a sale for 2 in West Oakland and one for a half on 35th Avenue. He lit a blunt and put the Black Street CD in. As soon as the song *Don't Go* came on, he started thinking about Tay. *Damn, I miss this bitch!* He picked the phone up and called her.

●●●●●●

The ringing of the phone woke Shaunté up. She hesitated to answer when she looked at the caller ID and saw Sin's mobile number.

"Hello!" she answered.

"I need to talk to you," he said.

"Just leave me alone, Sin. You already made it clear that you and me ain't got nothing to do with each other anymore," she said and cried.

"Tay, go on with that shit! You know muthafuckin well I love you more than anything. I just ain't with that shit you with. This is the second time. You playing games with me that you would play with a sucka, and I'm far from that!"

"I did the shit for us!" she screamed.

"Muthafucka, you did that shit for yo' got damn self!" he yelled. "Look, can we talk or what?" he asked.

"I should be here," she said.

"Well, I should be there in like an hour," he said and hung up.

Shaunté got up and walked up the full-length mirror and stared at her reflection. She took the short blue nightie off and rubbed her stomach and smiled. *I know I'm pregnant. I haven't had a period in two months.* "Little One, your timing's not too good," she said as she walked to the bathroom and ran some bath water and added some strawberry bath oil. She looked at the blunt and decided not to smoke it. When the tub was filled she got in and relaxed.

●●●●●●

Sin went to the spot and got 7 ½ birds and went and made his sales. He then went to his mom's and tucked the money and got dressed. He put on his dark blue Pelle Pelle jean shorts, a dark blue Pelle Pelle sweater vest over a crisp white T-shirt, and his blue and white Nike Air Max. He took all his jewels off and put on the 2 carat pinky ring, the 2 carat diamond earrings, the small link bracelet, the Movado watch, and the gold link chain with the gold weed leaf. He sprayed on some Joop and looked in the mirror and was satisfied with what he saw.

As he was on his way out the door his, mom came out the kitchen.

"Be here tomorrow. I'm cooking for Memorial Day," she said. Sin almost forgot tomorrow was the 28th.

"Oh, and someone named Mario called you yesterday. He said he would call you around 11:30 today and asked me to make sure you stayed here," she said.

"Ma, just give him my mobile number," he said and kissed her and left.

While Sin was on the freeway he called Tracy.

"Hello!" a male answered.
"Tracy there?"

"Who's this?" the dude asked.

"Sin," he said.

"Boo, your babies' daddy's on the phone," the dude yelled. Tracy picked up the upstairs extension.

"I got it!" she yelled. The dude hung up.

"What's up?" she asked.

"I'm about to come pick the kids up today."

"I'm about to take them to the mall. Meet us at Bayfair at 11:30 in Footlocker," she said.

"A'ight," Sin said and hung up.

When Sin got to the gates at Tay's house some chick was pulling out. She smiled and winked at Sin and he motioned her to give up the number. She raised her hand up and showed him her wedding ring. Sin rolled his window down and she did the same.

"Baby, I ain't tryin to step on your dude's toes. I'm just tryin to be your friend, you feel me?"

"Nah, baby. I ain't feeling that. We couldn't *just* be friends. You got a woman anyway. I be seeing her riding that car sometimes," she said.

"Well at least tell me your name."

"Yolanda Davis."

"Well look, Yolanda Davis. Can I get an e-mail address, or a pager number?" he asked.

"I see you're persistent. Give me your e-mail address."

"My hook up is lickyaright@aol.com," he said and smiled.

Hmm I bet, she thought. "Okay, Mr. Lick me right. What's your name?" she asked.

"Simian," he said and pulled off. When Sin got to the back he parked in visitors' parking. He looked around and got out the SS and pulled this phone out and called Tay.

Shaunté was sitting on her bed putting lotion on her legs when the house phone rang.

"Hello!" she answered.

"I'm at the door," Sin said.

"Here I come," she said and hung up. She picked up the fluffy green towel and wrapped it around herself and went and opened the door. Sin saw her standing there in the towel looking overly sexy. He walked in and went and sat on the baby blue leather love seat.

"So what was you fixing to do when you pulled up on me yesterday?" he asked.

"I was fixing to let you and that smart mouth bitch have it," she said seriously.

"Man, you brought all this shit on yourself."

"I don't feel like talking about that shit. Will you do me a favor?" she asked.

"What?"

"Put some lotion on my back?" she asked. Sin nodded his head and she went to the room.

When Tay came back in she was opening the bottle and dropped the top on the floor. She handed Sin the bottle and dropped the towel.

"You hungry?" she asked. Sin looked at her naked body. *I'm not supposed to be wanting to fuck this girl. I'm suppose to be kickin' her ass.*

"Nope, I already ate."

"Oh, your little bitch cooked for you?"

"Please believe it," he said as he squirted lotion into his hands and rubbed it on her shoulders and back. He then put some more on his hands and slowly massaged her ass, and between her thighs.

"I'll give you your props, she was cute," Shaunté said as she walked out of his reach.

Shaunté bent over and picked up the lotion top and Sin saw nothing but naked pussy from the back.

"I'm gone. You ain't playing fair," he said. Shaunté sat down across from him on the love seat.

"What's wrong, she ain't fucking you right?" she asked as she caressed her titties and pinched her nipples. She licked her right nipple and Sin almost busted out his shorts.

Shaunté knew he couldn't resist her. She opened her legs and let her hand roam down her body.

"Nah, Boo you're just used to me. Ain't that right, daddy?" she asked in her sexy voice as she sensually rubbed her clit. Sin got up and walked over to the love seat and stood in front of her. Shaunté put her foot on his chest. He kissed it, then her ankle, and between her thighs.

"Why you playin'?" he asked.

"I'm not!" she said. Shaunté stood up and her pussy was right in his face. He moved around her and sat in the love seat.

Shaunté pulled Sin's shorts and boxers down around ankles and straddled him and lowered herself down on him. She started riding him hard and making funny faces.

"Daddy, I'm sorry. Can I please have another chance?" she begged.

"I'm not tryin to get back in a relationship right now, with nobody," he said as he held her hips.

"Sin, you can see whoever you want to. I know how the game go. I fucked up! I just want to be the wife like I've been. I love you, and I'll do whatever to have you back in my life," she said.

"Anything?" Sin asked as he grinded her.

"Anything, I swear!" she moaned. Sin knew she was about to come, and knew it would be the right time to hit her off with what he was thinking.

"I want you to eat some pussy," he said as he started pounding harder.

"Oh baby, I'm about to come!" she screamed. Sin got her to the height of her nut and slowed down.

"What you doing?" she asked as she tried to grind herself on him harder. He held her right where she was.

"Answer me," he said as he licked her nipples.

"Whose?" she gasped.

"Juanda's."

"Yes. Now finish!" she whined.

Sin put her legs on his shoulder and grabbed her ass and fucked her hard. Shaunté wrapped her legs around his neck and fucked him back. After fifteen minutes Shaunté came hard. Sin came three seconds after her. He served her so good she cried. He pulled out of her and went to the bathroom and washed up.

"I suppose you want me to hook up your little freak session," she said as she came into the bathroom glowing.

"Fa sheezy!"

"You gonna come home tonight?" she asked.

"Nope, I gotta date," he said as he pulled his shorts and boxers up."

Shaunté frowned. "I hope your ass using rubbers!" she said angrily.

"And I hope you using them too, and that you ain't sucking nigga's dicks."

"Nigga, I was in Reno getting my pussy ate with the lights off. I didn't fuck that sucka or even entertain the thought of sucking dick," she said seriously. Sin knew she was telling the truth. One thing about Tay was for certain; she wouldn't lie to Sin about anything. If she was in the wrong she would tell the truth and suffer the consequences.

"I'm out," he said and kissed her on the mouth and left. He drove straight to San Leandro where Bay Fair was located.

When Sin walked in Footlocker every guy in there was looking at Tracy. She was wearing tight blue guess shorts, a white wife beater, and some white K-Swiss with no socks. The only jewels she had on was a blue Guess watch and a link chain with a gold heart locket with the kids pictures in it. Tracy was the second girl Sin had ever fell in love with. Malika was the first, and the one that hurt the most. Because he was only 16 when they were forced apart, it messed Sin up.

Tracy was a Sports Medicine Therapist at the San Lorenzo Sports Medicine Center. She worked on athletes that played for the Oakland A's, Oakland Raiders, and Golden State Warriors. She made good money. Sin used to tease her and say she was a high priced masseuse.

In all actuality though, Tracy was Sin's anchor. Anytime he was in trouble she was there. The only reason they broke up was because Tracy didn't want him selling dope anymore. At that time Sin was winning for real. He was getting a lot of money in Oakland, Pittsburg California, Reno, and Sacramento. She ended up getting pregnant again when Malik was 2 and didn't tell him. She had an abortion. What made him find out about the abortion was when he found a paper about it two weeks later. He went smooth off on her.

He met Yvette that night and started messing with her that week. He never stopped loving Tracy though, and even after he got with Yvette he still tipped with Tracy. He just couldn't be with her because he thought he couldn't trust her.

"Daddy!" Busy screamed and ran to him. Sin bent down and scooped him and hugged him.

Tracy said, "I'm so pissed off. They had the Jordan's in Busy's size but not Quesha's. I gotta go way to Richmond to Hilltop. The lady at the Footlocker is holding them for me," she said.

"What's it gon' take for you to let me have my way with you?" he asked.

"Not much," she said and turned around and kissed him on the lips. "Me and my co-workers going to Reno next week. You would wanna slide through," she said.

"We'll see," he said as he pulled a wad of cash out his pocket and peeled $400 off for himself and gave Tracy the rest.

"That's $2,100. I'll give you some more next week," he said.

"I didn't expect anything," she said.

"You wifey. You know I gotta break bread with you," he said.

Sin noticed a dude staring at Tracy as if he wasn't there.

He gritted his teeth.

"Nigga, you don't see me standing here or something?" he asked.

The dude's homeboy walked over. "What that fool say?" his boy asked.

He had a little size on him, but Sin wasn't intimidated. Sin raised his shirt and let the 9mm be seen. "Nigga, I'm talking about a problem. You want one?" he asked. The dudes hurried out of the store.

"That's the shit that broke us up! What if them niggas come back in here shooting? You don't ever think about the consequences to your actions!" Tracy said angrily.

"Man, I ain't tryin to hear that shit. If a broad was gawking at me your ass would pull a nutty, and anyway, where's my daughter?" he said.

"Busy, go get your sister out the toy store and tell her to come on," Tracy said. Busy ran across the way to the toy store as Quesha was coming out with a bag. She came over.

"Hi, Daddy!" she said and stood up on her tiptoes signaling a kiss. Sin leaned over and kissed her on the cheek.

"Hey, princess!" he said.

They were on their way to the exit when Sin looked in Oxford Street. He saw a light blue leather Pelle Pelle jacket and had to have it.

He walked into the Arab ran store and went to the

counter. "Man, what's up with the blue leather jacket, the matching jeans, the white name brand T-shirt, and some tan Tim's?" Sin asked.

"I got a good deal for you, cousin. Give me $500," the Arab said.

"Man, what the fuck you mean 'deal'? The jacket's $300, the jeans $70, the T-shirt's $30, and the boots are $100. Where's the deal?"

"No tax, cousin," he said.

"Nigga, you ain't my fuckin cousin. My cousin wouldn't be trying to get me like that."

"Give me $425. Only $25 for the boots," he said.

"That's what I'm talking about, my nigga!" Sin said as he shook dude's hand and gave him a ghetto hug. The dude went to the racks and got all Sin's sizes.

"Daddy, is that man our cousin?" Malik asked.

"No, stupid. That's just slang for a friend," Marquesha said. Tracy started laughing.

"What's slang for getting your butt whupped for calling your brother stupid?" she asked.

"Girl you call that boy stupid again I'm gon kick your ass!" Quesha said, imitating Tracy. Sin and Tracy started laughing. When the dude came with Sin's stuff he paid him with his new Visa Gold card.

As they were leaving the store a couple of cute women were passing by and one of them smiled at Sin and Tracy went off.

"What you looking at, you ugly bitch? If these kids wasn't here I'd beat your ass!" Tracy said. Sin pulled her by the arm.

"What's that shit? You just got on me for the same thing!" he said.

"I don't care," she said. Sin just shook his head and led the kids to the SS. They got in and he pulled off. He called Sheree as he got on 880.

"Hello!" she answered. Sin heard a lot of voices in the background.

"What's up?" he asked.

"Hi, honey! What you doing?"

"Nothing. I have some people I want you to meet."

"Where are you?"

"I'm on the freeway on my way to Footlocker in Hilltop."

"I'll be up there in 20 minutes. I need to finish baking this cake (cooking the dope)."

"A'ight," he said and hung up.

Chapter Seven

The Hookup

When Sin got to El Cerrito his phone rang.

"Hello!" he answered.

"Sin, this is Mario. What up?"

"What up, boy?" Sin asked in Spanish.

"Man, call my sister, Maria. I got something for you," he said.

While Sin was in a holding cell in one of the Atlanta police stations, he saw some white boys plotting on Mario. He noticed the XIV tattoo on Mario's arm. That tattoo meant that he was from Northern Cali, and Oakland's in Northern Cali. When two of the eight white boys pushed up on Mario, Sin got close.

"I'm not going to tell you again, give me a fuckin cigarette, you fuckin spick," one of them said.

"Where you from?" Sin asked him in Spanish.

"Stockton, Cali," Mario said.

"I'm from Oakland. I got your back."

Mario was a dark Puerto Rican. He could pass for black mixed with Indian. The other six white boys got up looking crazy at Sin. The seven blacks in the cell got up when they peeped what was going on. Sin looked at Mario.

"It's on you," he said in Spanish. Mario pulled back and busted the biggest dude's eye open. Sin hit the other one and knocked him out. He then helped Mario with the big dude. When he fell, they stomped him unconscious and the other white boys couldn't do anything but watch.

Mario also had a gun case, but they went in his house illegally and found the gun. He lost in trial and got served with sixteen years. He and Sin went to prison together and they ended up in the same cell and ended up being good friends. You hardly ever saw one without the other.

Mario had a chick out there, named Brandy, that he was seeing and she hooked Sin up with her cousin, Michelle. Sin and Michelle didn't hit it off that well. He felt every time she came to see him she had an attitude.

"So what's up man? You a'ight?" Sin asked.

"I'm good. How you doing out there?" he asked.

"Nigga, I'm starving," Sin said.

"Call my sister. It's all good. So what you been up to?

"Surviving."

"Don't trip, it's going to get better, trust me. Did you catch up with the Yvette bitch about your loot and yours cars?"

"Yeah, I twisted that hoe outta damn near 100 gees, and somebody set the Benz on fire. It's cool though. I'm getting the money back from the insurance. I still got my K5, and I let her keep the Camaro," Sin said. They both started laughing.

"Oh yeah, Michelle said to tell you to give her a call," he said.

"Shit! When they came to see us that bitch was acting like it wasn't cool."

"You know broads play hard to get sometimes."

"A'ight, give me your sister's number. I know Michelle's." Mario read the number off and Sin programmed it into his phone.

"Say, man I gotta go. I'll holla at you later," he said.

"A'ight," Sin said and hung up.

Sin called Maria after he changed CD's.

"Hello!" she answered.

"May I speak to Maria?" he asked.

"This is she."

"This is Sin. Your brother told me to call you."

"I been waiting two months for you to call."

"I been kinda busy." *Damn she sound hella good,* Sin thought.

"Can you come to Lodi tomorrow?" she asked.

"Yeah, when and where?" She read off her address.

"Look, baby. I can't remember all that. I'll call you when I get out there tomorrow at 2."

"I'll see you then," she said.

"Maria, one more thing."

"Yes?"

"What you look like?" he asked. She started laughing.

"I'm 5'3", 260 pounds, with braces," she said.

Damn, 5'3", 260? I'm cool on that there.

"A'ight, I'll holla at you tomorrow," he said and hung up quickly.

When they got to Hilltop Mall there were top notch women everywhere. The kids helped Sin get many numbers. Women were stopping him with the "Oh, are these your kids?" "They're so cute!" and "Hey daddy"'s.

When they got to Footlocker, he paid for Quesha's shoes and bought them 3 more pairs each, compliments of Visa.

Sheree walked in and all eyes were on her.

"Hey!" she said and kissed him.

"Daddy, who's that?" Quesha asked as she protectively took his hand.

"This is my girlfriend, Sheree," Sin said.

"I thought Shaunté was your girlfriend," Malik said.

"They are so cute," Sheree said as she sat down in front of Quesha. "What's your name, pretty?" she asked.

"Marquesha."

"My name is Malik, but you can call me Busy," Busy said as he bumped Quesha out of the way.

"You are so handsome," Sheree said as she kissed him on the cheek. She looked up at Sin. "So are you staying the night?" she asked.

"Yeah, for sure that!" Sin said as they all walked out the store. Sheree was wearing some light blue DKNY denim Capri's, a white DKNY baby tee, and some white and blue DKNY slip on sneakers. Dudes were literally bumping into stuff trying to get a look at her. Sin was really feeling his oats, because he had her, and everybody wanted her.

"Come on, lunch on me!" she said. She put one arm around Sin and held Busy's hand with the other. Sin put one around Sheree and the other around Quesha. They went and had Chinese food.

"So, what you and the little ones about to do?" she asked.

"I'm taking them to the Discovery Zone," he said. "I'm going to buy you a few things for my house then, I'm going to handle my business.

"Oh yeah? Bring me one of them thangs when you come home," she said as she kissed him on the lips.

"A'ight, I'll be there at 10."

"I'll see you guys later," she said to the kids and left. Sin took the kids' hands and they cut.

●●●●●●

Sin took the kids home at 7:00. He hadn't met Tracy's dude since he had been home. When he pulled up to her house there was a purple 97 Mustang convertible GT parked next to Tracy's Camry. He got the kids' stuff out the trunk and walked up to the door. He rang the bell, and a big light skinned cat opened it. He was 5'11" and 190 pounds of solid muscle. He had dark brown eyes, a short 'fro, and Tattoos all over his arms. The kids walked in and Sin followed them. They went to their rooms and Sin stood there. The dude sized Sin up.

"What's up man? I'm Sin."

"What's up with you and my woman?" he asked. Sin saw fear in the dude.

"Man, don't be questioning me about Tracy. What she tell you was up with us?" Sin asked.

"She says ain't nothing up. I'm just saying, the collect calls, visits, and packages, that shit adds up," he said.

Sin was pissed. *This nigga is a straight bitch!* Just then Tracy came downstairs.

"Man, where you find this insecure cat at?" Sin asked her.

"So, you gon' answer me, or what?" the dude asked Sin.

"I'll tell you like this, *potna.* If I was trying to get her back, I'd have her, and your ass would be out," Sin said. The dude started walking up to Sin and Tracy got in the middle.

"Ya'll ain't fixing to start this shit while my kids in here!" she said.

Sin pointed up. "Nigga, you better thank God my kids is up there. I swear on they lives, if they *wasn't*, I'd whack your punk ass!" Sin said as he turned to leave.

Tracy looked at her boyfriend and followed Sin outside.

"Man, that fool even *act* like he wanna get outta pocket, call me!" he said.

"I'm moving out of here. Since you been out, he been acting like when I ain't here I'm creeping with you," she said.

"So, we still on for Friday?" He asked.

"Yes."

"Don't give that nigga no loving. I'm trying to suck on that coochie while we out there," he said as he got in the SS and cut.

Sin had a few sales and went and took care of them. He then went to North Oakland and shot dice with a few cats he knew. He won about 5 gees and left. He went to the spot and got a key of dope for Sheree. Sin called her when he got to her house. She buzzed the gate and he pulled in and parked next to her Cherokee. He got out and grabbed his gun, clothes, and the key. When he got to the door Sheree was wearing a blue extra large men's long sleeve button up and a pair of white Nike ankle socks.

Sin stepped in and kissed her.

"Are you hungry, baby?" she asked as she took his jacket and hung it up.

"Starving!" he said as he handed her the bag with the dope in it. Sheree went out the sliding glass door to the balcony and hid the key.

"Sit down and I'll make you a plate," she said.

Sin put the 9mm on the table in the hall and went in the bathroom and washed his hands. When he came back Sheree handed him a plate of catfish and garlic crab. He devoured it. When he was done Sheree cleared the table then went to the bathroom and ran him a bath. She put rose petals in the water and lit some candles. She went back to the living room and grabbed her weed box and rolled a blunt, then went to the kitchen and grabbed a bottle of Hypnotiq.

"Come on, baby," she said as she pulled him up. She walked him to the bathroom and he saw the roses in the water. *This girl's something else!* He got undressed, and when he got his boxers off, Sheree smiled.

"I see you working with a lil' somethin' somethin'," she said as she popped him on the ass. He got in and Sheree got on her knees and started washing him up.

"You ain't gonna get in with me?" he asked.

"You want me too?" Sin nodded his head.

Sheree got up and went to her bedroom and lay out her short red nightie. She went to the living room and got both their phones. She came back into the bedroom and slid her socks and blue thong off. When she came into the bathroom she was unbuttoning her shirt. When she came out of it Sin was sprung for real. She got in the tub and sat with her back against his chest. Sheree lit the blunt and passed it to him.

"I can get used to this," he said.

"That's what I want you to do," she said as she hit the drink straight from the bottle.

Sin passed her the blunt. He hit the drink then kissed her on the neck.

"What's up? Can a cat make love to you tonight?" he asked.

"You could've made love to me this morning before you left. I said I don't have sex on the *first day*. That was yesterday. This morning was another day, and if you keep kissing my neck it's going to be on," she said. Sin sucked on her ear and she sighed. Just then her phone rang.

"Hello!" she said in a sexy voice.

"What up, baby?" a male voice asked.

"Man, what you want? I have a man and it ain't cool for you to be calling here," she said to her ex friend, Mike.

"Bitch, what? Don't make me come over there!" he threatened.

"Nigga, you come over here with that shit it's going to be problems," she said and hung up. "That nigga know he ain't got nothing coming. When I'm through with a nigga, I'm through for good," she said.

Sin's phone rang.

"What's up?" he asked.

"What's up, Cuzzo?" Rod asked.

"What's cracking, Cuzzo?"

"Everything looking cool?" Rod asked.

"I'm done, man."

"That's cool. I talked to my hook up and he hollering it's a drought. Man, what's up with you and your girl? I called there and she said you left her. Where you staying at?" Rod asked.

"At mom's."

"That ain't cool. You can stay at the under spot. I got another one in Fremont."

"Cool. When you coming back, Cuzzo?" Sin asked.

"Friday,"

"A'ight, Cuzzo" Sin said as he tickled Sheree.

She giggled. "Stop!" she said.

"Where, you at?" Rod asked.

"At Sheree's" Sin said.

"What! How you manage that?"

"Come on, man you know my work. I'll holla," Sin said and hung up.

Sin washed Sheree's back and she washed his. They both bathed then got out. They lotioned each other down and got dressed for bed. Sheree straddled Sin's back and gave him a massage. Sin then gave her one. They were laying down kissing when there was a loud knock at the door. They both frowned.

"Who the fuck's at my door this late at night?" she said. She got up grabbed her robe and the 9mm out of the night stand drawer and went to the front door.

"Who is it? she asked.

"Mike!" he yelled. Sheree went back to the room.

"Come in here with me. This muthafucka likes to act ignorant," she said. Sin got up and put on his shorts and shoes and grabbed his gun off the night stand. They went to the door as Mike banged again.

Sin opened the door and came face to face with a big ugly dude. He was like 6'6" and 265 pounds. He was light skinned, had gray eyes, long sandy brown braids, and a monstrous face. Sin made sure to keep his gun behind the door.

"What's up, man?" he asked.

"Let me holla at ol' girl," Mike said.

"Look here, folks. She ain't trying to holla at you. I ain't trying to play super hero or nothing like that, but you fucking off what I'm trying to do, for real. Holla at her tomorrow, on *her* time," Sin said. He could tell Mike was thinking about doing something, so he stepped to the side. Mike saw Sin's gun and saw Sheree standing behind Sin with a gun. He knew it was a no winner, so he left.

Sin closed and locked the door. He watched Sheree's ass bounce as he followed her back to the bedroom. He pulled her to him and started kissing on her neck and ear. Sheree unzipped his shorts and pulled them and his boxes down. Sin stepped out of them and untied Sheree's robe and slipped it off of her. He then took the nightie off of her and lay her back on the bed.

He kissed her from her ankles to her head. Sheree slipped the condom on him and guided him in. As soon as Sin broke skin he knew she had that fire. Sheree put her legs around his waist and he sexed her slow. The dick was feeling so good that Sin's slow stroking her made her dig her nails into his back. When Sin came, Sheree pulled him in until his dick hit the bottom.

"Damn, baby! You got it good!" Sheree moaned as she came.

Whey they were done Sheree lay there shaking from the after shock. *This nigga is a keeper*, she thought. They lay there for a few minutes, then Sheree went and washed up and came back in with a warm, soapy rag. After she cleaned Sin up she lay her head on his arm. Sin put his other hand on her ass and pulled her closer.

"So, where we gon take this?" he asked. Sheree's face was an inch from his as she looked in his eyes.

"I don't want to go too fast, Sin. Anytime I rush into anything, it don't come out right. I don't want that with us," she said.

That's what I'm saying! No strings is a good thing, Sin thought to himself. "I respect that, and I want to do whatever will make you comfortable."

"I will respect that we have an intimate relationship, and not sleep with anyone but you," she said.

I ain't about to do that. I ain't committed to nobody. I'm fuckin whoever, whenever, he thought. He kissed her on the lips and went to sleep.

When Sin got up the next morning it was 8:00. Sheree wasn't in the bed. He picked up the phone and saw he had one message. He checked it and it was Terell saying he was ready. Sheree came in the room and lay on top of him.

"You wanna eat?" she asked.

"After I get a little more of this bomb," he said as he opened her robe. She straddled him and slid down on his dick and rode him. They went at it for thirty minutes and he tried to pull out when his nut was coming, but Sheree wasn't going for that. She rode it all out of him.

She got up and ran in the bathroom and got in the shower. Sin went in there ten minutes later. Sheree got out and went and made his breakfast. When Sin got out the shower he saw his clothes laid out and ironed. He lotioned himself down then put on his blue silk boxers and went to the kitchen and ate the steak and egg breakfast.

When he was done, he brushed his teeth then got dressed. Sheree put his hat on his head backwards, gave him a blunt and picked up his backpack and handed him $500.

"That's what I owed you from Saturday, and this the $17,500 for the package you brought last night. Be careful, and call me sometime today to let me know you're okay," she said and kissed him.

"A'ight, I'm out."

Sin walked out and saw how nice a day it was and regretted not having a convertible. He threw the backpack and coat in the trunk and left. He hit the freeway and rolled the windows down and played the Nas' CD. He lit the blunt as the phone rang.

"What up?" he asked.

"Sin, this Bo. What's up?"

"Bo, what's cracking?"

"I'm trying to holla."

"Meet me at the spot I saw you at in 30 minutes," Sin said and hung up. He went to the spot grabbed the last key and a half, left the money and cut. He was going to give Bo the half on consignment. Bo had a spot in Berkeley that was knocking hard. He bought at least 18 ounces a day from Sin. His money just wasn't right. Sin figured he would help the dude get his loot right, and that would have Bo spending more with him. He called Terell to meet him there too.

When Sin pulled up at Eastmont Mall, he parked on the bottom on the side the movies were on. He saw Bo pull up in a blue Honda Accord. Bo came and got in the car. Sin handed him the dope.

"That's half a bird. Niggas talking about a drought. Give me 9 gees. If everything is cool, I'll give you a whole one next time. I would've done it this time but I only got one left and its Terell's," Sin said.

"You think you gonna have some more later? My spot is a straight machine. We do it 24."

"I don't know. If I do I'll call you before I leave town on my way home," Sin said. Terell and Déja pulled up in Déja's red 5.0. Bo got out of the car and Terell got in.

"Bro, I don't like that nigga. It's something that ain't cool about him," Terell said as he gave Sin the $17,500.

"It's a drought. Go up on ya'll ounces, Dump them for $750. I want $18,000 on the keys until I tell you its over. Ya'll should be able to make $9,000 profit."

"I'm coming by your mama's house later on. Save me some ribs," Terell said as he got out.

Sin hit the freeway to Lodi. As soon as he got to Castro Valley, the heat was killing him. He rolled the windows up and turned the A/C on and lit his blunt. As soon as he got to Lodi he called Maria.

"Hello!" she answered.

"Maria, this is Sin. I'm at the Shell gas station. How I get there?"

"Pull out the front of the station, go left and come down

to the third light. Make a right and come to the second stop sign. Make the right and drive down the street. My house is the one with the silver convertible Corvette parked in front, and the black Expedition in the driveway," she instructed him.

"Okay, here I come."

Sin pulled out of the gas station and followed the directions. When he pulled up at the little house, he got out and went to the door. When he got to the top of the stairs, the cutest Puerto Rican girl he had ever seen opened the door. She stood at 5'5" and weighed no more than 130 pounds. She had long black hair, green eyes, and a beautiful face. She favored the singer, Christina Milian. Her body was something else. She had 34DD titties which strained against the red Nike sports bra. She had sexy abs, a 24 inch waist, 40 inch hips, sexy thighs in the black Nike tights, and a nice puffy outline of her pussy.

"You're definitely not what I was expecting," Sin said.

"Neither are you," Maria replied with a smile. *Damn, he's fine!* she thought. "You have to excuse the way I'm looking. I just came back from the gym."

"Baby, you're interfering with God's greatest work by messing with that gym," Sin said.

"Thank you!"

Maria closed the door and turned and walked down the hallway. Sin looked at her ass and was mesmerized by how it bounced from left to right.

"Jesus!" he moaned.

"Huh?" she said as she stopped.

"Nothing."

Her phone rang as they came in the living room.

"Hello!" she answered.

"What's up? My potna get there yet?" Mario asked.

"Yeah, he just got here. Mario, he is *FINE*!" she said in Spanish.

"Baby sister, holla at him. He might be single."

"I don't care if he does have a woman. I'll snatch him from her," she said.

"Go get what I told you to give him and give him the phone."

"Your Dawg wants to holla at you," she said as she handed Sin the phone.

"So you wanna snatch me up, huh, beautiful?" he asked in Spanish."

"You speak Spanish!" she screamed. "I am so embarrassed!" she said as she got up.

"What's up, Dawg?" Sin said.

"My little sister likes you."

"I like her too, brother-in-law," Sin joked.

"So what you getting whole ones for?" he asked.

"Fifteen-5 each," Sin lied.

"My people got it for 15 year around. You handle something for us, I'll hook you up for 13-5. Ten if you get 10 or better," Mario said.

Maria came in and handed him a shopping bag. He looked in it and found a brick of coke wrapped in brown paper.

"Dawg, what's this for?" he asked.

"If it's what she gave you, it's for having my back the last four years," Mario said.

"So, what you want me to do?" he asked.

"My sis will tell you. I gotta go. I'll talk to you tomorrow. Let me holla back at my sis," he said.

Sin gave Maria the phone and did some math in his head. *If I use 100 gees of Rod's loot and buy 10 keys and sell them for 17-5 each, I can make like 75 gees for myself. I can do that a few times before Friday.*

"Take him to meet pops. Also talk to him about that shit with Don," Mario said to Maria.

"Okay," she said. They hung up.

"So, do you have a boyfriend?" Sin asked.

"I'm kinda seeing someone, but it's nothing serious. What about you?"

"I just started seeing someone. It's really too soon to tell."

"Mario wants me to take you to see our dad." They stood up within an inch of each other.

"So, what's up? Can I take you out?" he asked.

"How about lunch tomorrow."

"That's cool."

Maria grabbed a Coach bag and her keys. They went outside and got in the Corvette. Maria put a red Nike windbreaker on.

"My father thinks that I dress too sexy," she said as she started the car and pulled off.

"If you got it, baby, floss it!" Sin said. Maria turned the A/C on full blast.

"You got any kids?" she asked.

"Yeah, I have a 7 year old son and a 9 year old daughter."

"I want some kids," she said. They pulled into the parking lot of a Mexican restaurant called Angelina's. Maria parked and they got out and went in.

"Hey, Papi!" Maria said to an older, well built Hispanic man.

"Hey, baby!" he said and kissed her.

"This is Mario's friend, Simian. He's the one that was

there with him in Atlanta. Sin, this my dad, Big Mario," she said. They shook hands.

"My friend, I'm forever in your debt," Big Mario said. They all sat down and ate and talked for almost an hour. Big Mario saw that Maria was digging Sin. When they got up and were leaving, he stopped Maria.

"You like Simian, baby?" he asked in Spanish.

"Yeah, he's cool."

Big Mario laughed and kissed her as she was leaving. He rushed to the back office to make a call. He was going to have Sin thoroughly checked out. He had built his empire from the ground up and couldn't risk being infiltrated by an outsider.

Sin and Maria pulled up in her driveway.

"What's up? Can I come back out here later on and spend $100,000?" he asked.

"Yeah, it's all good, but you gotta come to the restaurant. We're having a family party," Maria told him as they got out of the car.

"Is 9 cool?" he asked. "Damn, it's hot!" Sin said as he took his T-shirt off.

Maria stared at Sin's cut up muscles and felt herself getting wet. *I want to fuck*, she thought. "Yeah, that's fine," she said.

"Now about the other thing. This punk, named Don, owes us 500 grand, and since Mario's in jail, he thinks he don't have to break bread. My dad and uncle have so much money they ain't trippin' on it. It's the principle though. He gets away, everyone else will try. He's got money. I found out he recently got 50 keys from the Colombians," Maria said, trying to keep her eyes off Sin's chest.

"Does he have a family?"

"Yeah, he has a wife and kids. You keep half the money for yourself, and under no circumstances do the kids get hurt," she said.

"I'll handle it tonight. I'll see you later on," he said and rubbed her cheek.

Sin walked over to the SS and put his shirt on the hot leather seat. He picked the phone up and called Sheree.

"Hello!" she answered.

"Baby, what you doing today?" he asked.

"Probably nothing. What's up?"

"I wanna show you off. You wanna come to my mom's? She's cooking."

"Yeah!" she said. Sin gave her the directions.

He then went to his mom's and got all his clothes and went to the spot. Once everything was in place, he went and got his money from Terell. He then went to Berkeley and got his money from Bo. As Sin was pulling off, his phone rang. He looked at the caller ID and saw Shaunté's number.

"Hello!" he answered.

"Sin, I need a whole one," she said.

"I'll be there in a minute," he said and hung up.

Sin saw Lisa and Déja's cars when he got to Shaunté's. When he came in he saw Juanda there also.

"Shit! The reason I ain't seen no dimes out today is because they all up in here," he said as he kissed all of them on their cheeks.

"What you so happy about?" Shaunté asked.

"Come in the room so I can holla at you," he said.

They walked into the room and Shaunté closed the door. Sin sat on the bed.

"Rod called me and said his hook up is talking about a drought."

"Tone, from 94th called me saying he needed something. He asked if our prices were what everyone else's were. When I asked what that was, he told me 20 gees," she said.

"I got a hook up for 10 a key. I'm going to use Rod's money and get 10 and keep selling them for 17-5. That's $175,000 every 10 keys. Seventy-five thousand is all us. If anybody in The Circle want 10 or better, I'll drop it to 15 a key. I need you to help me on this shit and we can split the money. You down?" Sin asked.

"Hell yeah!" Shaunté replied.

"So what Juanda out here for?" he asked.

"She want to get one. She came out here with some nigga she left at the hotel. They driving back tonight," she said.

"Shit! We can't serve her and Tone. This is thc last one," he said.

"Tone was just trying to see what our prices were. How much you gonna sell that one to Juanda for?" she asked.

"Seventeen-five, you could have that. I need you to go with me to Tracy's later on, about 8:30," he said.

"Sin, I'm miserable and I can't sleep right without you next to me."

Sin kissed her on the head. "You should've thought about that before you fucked over me," he said as he walked out the room.

"I'll see ya'll later," he said.

"So what we suppose to do in the meantime?" Shaunté asked.

"Shit! Shut shop down until tomorrow. Just keep putting the word out that our prices still the same and we'll be ready in the morning," he said as he walked out.

Chapter Eight

A Favor 4 A Favor

Sin was in his mom's backyard sitting at the table when June, his wife Latoya, their two kids, and June's oldest daughter Shamika came.

"What's up, Uncle?" Shamika said.

"What's up, Lil' Diamond?" Sin said and kissed her cheek. When Sin was 15, he and Malika had their own apartment, three cars, and big money. Simone, Shamika's mom, had Shamika when she was 16. Sin nicknamed her Lil' Diamond. When Sin wasn't in the street, he and Malika were keeping Shamika. She was his favorite niece.

Shamika went into the house to see her grandmother and June walked up.

"You holla at Rod?" he asked. Sin nodded as he sipped his water.

"He tell you they talking about a drought?"

"Yeah, but now I got another connection that's only charging me 15 a bird if I buy 10 or better. If not, they're 17-5."

"Shit, 17-5 is still cool. Javier and Gabe talking about 20, Sin. If the shit cool, put me an order in for 25 of them muthafuckas," he said. Sin was going to tell June to fuck his self, but thought better of it.

"A'ight, I got you. Meet me on the block in the morning so you can see what the shit look like," he told him.

Tracy and the kids arrived and came over to Sin. Sin was playing dominoes with June against their twin cousins, Freddy and Teddy.

"Sheree!" Malik yelled and ran over to her. Sin turned and looked and saw Sheree standing by the gate. She was wearing a white and blue Nike polo shirt, a blue Nike tennis skirt, white Nike ankle socks, and some white and blue Air Max. She had her hair in Shirley Temple curls.

"Damn, who's that?" Teddy asked. June looked at Sin.

"Bro, she lookin' for you or Rod?" June asked.

"Me."

"Man, I know you ain't doing business outta mama's house," June said as Sheree walked up. Sin tilted his head up.

"Hey, honey!" she said and leaned down and kissed him. "What's up, June Bug?" She said.

"Sin, you be coming up on proper work," June said.

"Come on, baby. I want you to meet the queen," Sin said and walked her into the house and introduced her to his mom and aunties. They walked back outside and sat down.

"You hungry?" she asked. Sin looked at her thighs.

"Yeah, for sure that," he said. Sheree started blushing.

"Stop being nasty around the kids," she whispered in his ear. Just then, Tracy walked up.

"Are you going to introduce me to your friend?" she asked.

"Sheree, this is Malik and Quesha's mama, Tracy. Tracy, this is my girl, Sheree," Sin said. They exchanged hellos then Sheree went and made their plates. Tracy looked at Sin.

"So, are ya'll in something serious?" she asked. Sin knew he had to stroke Tracy's ego.

"Come on now, baby. You know the only woman I was ever serious about was you," he said. *This nigga thinks he's so smooth*, she thought.

"You just make sure you in Reno after midnight Friday, and the dick and tongue is working properly," she said.

"You make sure the head, pussy, and asshole's right," he responded. Sheree brought their plates and they ate.

Sin knew the day was too good to be true when he saw Yvette come storming through the gate and towards them. *Shit!* he thought.

"I want my muthafuckin' money, Sin!" she yelled. Sin had never hit Yvette, but he was about to knock her out right then.

"Bitch, I don't owe you shit. That $96,000 was the $50,000 you got me for, and the other $46,000 was for pain, suffering, and interest. So chalk that to the game," he said.

"Hold on, bitch! You don't be bringing that shit to my mama house!" June yelled.

"Don't tell her nothing. I'm gon' beat her ass! Shamika

take all the kids in the house," Tracy said.

"Fuck what ya'll going through! I want my money, and I want it now!" she yelled as she stuck her finger in Sin's face. Sin was just about to hit her but Sheree reacted. She pushed Yvette's hand and stood up.

"Bitch, back your scandalous ass up off my man before I do something to you!" she said.

Sin had enough. He pushed Yvette real hard and she fell on her ass. He stood up and snatched her up by the shirt and pushed her toward the house.

"Baby, no!" Sheree said and tired to follow. Tracy got in front of her and stopped her.

"You don't know the scoop on that. Sit down and I'll explain it to you," she said.

Sin pulled Yvette into his room and locked the door. He then turned and slapped her so hard she rolled over the bed and landed on the floor on the other side.

"Bitch, you think that shit you pulled out there was *fly*? Hoe, did you see my mama, my kids, and the rest of my fam' out there?" Sin yelled.

Yvette got up and ran up on Sin. He side stepped the wild punches she was throwing and grabbed the front of her shirt and slammed her against the wall hard. When Yvette hit the wall all the fight was gone out of her.

"You wanna be talking about *your* money! What about the 50 gees you twisted *me* out of?" he yelled.

"What the fuck was I suppose to do? You left me by myself. You told me they were trying to give you 30 years! I couldn't wait," she said.

"It ain't even about you leaving. You didn't have to take the money I was risking *my* freedom to get. You didn't even wait until I was sentenced. You didn't even come see me once. Then you got pregnant by and married the next nigga," Sin yelled and hit the wall overhead.

"Sin, the baby's yours! Her name is Simara."

Sin thought about the picture of the little girl on the mantle at Yvette's house.

"I ain't trying to hear that shit! If that was my kid why you ain't let June know? When you saw Tracy at Hot August Nights, why didn't you tell her? What is this, a plot to get me to break off some loot?" he asked.

Yvette wasn't a liar and Sin knew that, but the thought of her having his kid, and keeping it on the under was unbelievable. Still, she may have been scandalous as far as running off with the money, but she wasn't a liar.

"Sin, I'm not lying, and I ain't here to get you to take care of Simara. I'm here because James pissed me off and I told him I set the lick up, and it was you that robbed us. Me and Maira are staying at my mom's. I don't have anywhere else to go. I want to move to Reno where my job has another branch. I need some money to relocate."

"Stay right here. I'll be right back," he said and walked out and down the hall.

Sin went to his sister's old room and locked the door. He went in the closet and moved the hanging clothes, pulled out the wall paneling and there was a wall safe. He opened it and counted the rubberband bound stacks of money. There were 10. Every stack was $10,000. He counted out 5 gees. *I got 95 racks left,* he thought.

Sin locked the safe and put everything back as it was then went back to his room. He handed Yvette the money.

"I need a blood test. If Simara's my daughter, I'll step up," he said. Yvette tried to kiss him and he stepped back.

"Yvette, I feel like killing you for real. Don't push your luck. And you fixing to go out there and apologize to my fam," he said. They walked out and Yvette walked over to Sin's mom.

"Miss Jackie, I'm sorry for disrespecting your house. Your son made me lose my temper," she said and kissed her on her cheek.

"It's okay, baby. His daddy used to make me lose mine. I know how it is." Moms said. Yvette then left.

"What happened?" Sheree asked when Sin sat down. He kissed her cheek.

"I might have another daughter," he said.

Everybody kicked it and had fun. At 8:00 everybody started leaving.

"I'll see you when you get home," Sheree said as she kissed him. She got in her Cherokee and left. Sin went in the house and got $100,000 of Rod's money and left, and went to the spot and waited for Tay.

At 9:00, Sin was dressed in black cargo sweats, a black T-shirt, a black hoodie, and some black Tim's. He remembered he had to go in Maria's restaurant and hurried to changed back. When he heard Tay pull up he grabbed his blacks, the Mack-11, and the 100 gees and went to the door. When he opened it Shaunté was standing there in a blue silk slip dress and some blue suede open toed six inch heels.

"Come on, we running late," he said as he locked up and they went to the Yukon.

Shaunté handed him the keys and they got in and rode out. Sin told Shaunté what happened with Yvette.

"I started to come over there. I would've fucked that bitch up. So what you gonna do about the little girl?"

"I can't do nothing but wait to take the blood test," he said as he lit a blunt. He hit it and passed it. He looked down at Shaunté's thighs and felt himself getting hard. Shaunté saw the bulge in his pants as she passed the weed back.

"Is this for me?" she asked as she rubbed his dick.

"Not tonight," he said as he picked his phone up and called Maria.

"Hello!" she answered.

"Hey, this is Sin, I'm on my way."

"You're going to have to come in," she said.

"A'ight," he said and hung up.

"You lookin cool in that dress," he said to Shaunté.

"It's cool, but I don't like not wearing panties."

"You ain't got none on?" he asked.

"Nope," she said and raised the dress exposing herself.

"Tay, don't have me beat your ass."

"This ain't the kind of dress you wear panties with," she said.

When they got to Angelina's they parked and got out.

"Do I need my gun?" she asked.

"Nah, this ain't that type of party," he said as he grabbed her hand and they went in. There were a lot of people in there. He walked up to the table where Maria, her father and everyone else was sitting. Maria introduced him, and he introduced Shaunté.

"Shaunté, why don't you sit down and have a drink while I talk to Sin in the office," Maria said as she got up and gave Tay her chair. Tay looked at Sin and he nodded at her.

Sin followed Maria to the back. She had on a long gray silk dress and heels, which made her look even more sexy. Sin went out the back door and got the bag of money out the Yukon. He came back in and gave it to Maria.

"So, that's your girlfriend?" she asked.

"Something like that."

"She's cute. When you go see Don, make sure he knows you were sent by Mario," she said as she gave him the address and the directions.

"That dude that was sitting next to you, that's your dude?"

"Something like that," she said as she pointed to a box. Sin picked it up and she followed him outside to the Yukon.

"Sometimes I'm early getting where I'm going. So if you're still in the bed when I get there it's more than okay," he said and smiled at her.

What is it about this man that makes me want him so bad? "That can be misconstrued as something else. I *have* been drinking," she said. Sin stared at her for a second.

"Can I show you something?" he asked.

"Show me," she said. Sin pulled her to him and kissed her neck and shoulder.

"Mmm," she moaned.

"You like that?" he softly asked in her ear.

"Keep going," she sighed. Sin licked from her chin, down her neck, to her cleavage. He licked her exposed chest, and the inside of her cleavage. Maria's hand crept down and she grabbed his dick. Sin kissed back up to her mouth and her lips parted and they tongued. Sin grabbed a handful of ass and realized Maria didn't have panties on. He let out a breath and backed away from her.

"You're addictive," he said.

"Simian, you shouldn't start fires you're not going to put out," she pouted.

"I'll be by tomorrow," he said.

"I'm telling you now, I'm a freak."

"Shit! Well, we gon' have fun," he said.

Maria picked up a napkin and wet it and wiped her lipstick off his face. She opened her purse and put more on her lips. They went back in the dining room and there were a few guys around Shaunté. She was the center of attention. They said their goodbyes and left. Big Mario came up to Maria.

"Is he gonna take care of you and your brother's little problem?" he asked.

"Yes, Papi, he's going to handle it."

"If he does good we'll see if he wants to handle *our* big problem," Big Mario said and walked away. Just then Maria's cousin, Shauna, walked over.

"Ria, who's that guy you were with?" she asked.

"That's Mario's friend. And before you ask for the hook up, I'm already at him," Maria said.

When Sin and Shaunté pulled up on Don's block, they

drove by like they were merely going down the street.

"Did you notice anything?" she asked as he pulled over.

"Nah, it look straight. You ready?" he asked.

"You know it," she said as she pulled her dress over her head leaving her in nothing but her blue strapless bra. Sin just stared. "Daddy, come on! We don't have time for that," she said as she leaned over the seat and grabbed her bag. She put on the blue thong panties, the black cargo sweats, the bulletproof vest, her black hoodie, and all black Jordan's.

As Sin got dressed she put her hair in a ponytail and put her mask on her head so it looked like a beanie. Sin loaded and cocked the Mac 11. Tay checked her 9mm Taurus and cocked it.

"Let's make this shit happen. We ain't even gon' play with this cat. We gon' get this money or we fixing take this sucka and kill him," Sin said as they walked down the street. When they got to the door, Shaunté rang the bell as Sin stood to the side out of sight.

"Yes!" a female answered.

"My car broke down outside. Can I please use your phone?" Shaunté whined. The woman looked out the window and saw Shaunté standing there looking scared. She unlocked and opened the door and came face to face with the barrel of Shaunté's 9. Sin pulled his mask down and stepped out into the open.

"Just be quiet and everything will be fine. Where's Don?" he asked in Spanish. She pointed to the family room.

"Please don't hurt my kids!" she pleaded.

"As long as Don give me the money, everything will be good, I promise," Sin said.

They walked down the hall to the family room. Shaunté was the first one in. When Don saw her, he tried to go for a gun that was on the table. Sin already had his gun pointed at him. Shaunté moved faster than Sin could blink and slapped Don in the head with her gun then took his.

"We can make this easy or hard. Where's the money?" Shaunté asked.

"What money?" he asked.

Sin gently pushed the chick forward. He sat her on the sofa next to Don. He sat himself on a chair across from them and Tay stood behind them with her gun on the back of Don's head.

"So you want to play?" Sin asked Don. He looked at the cute Puerto Rican girl. "What's your name?" he asked.

"Bianca," she said.

"Well, Bianca, since he thinks we playing, I gotta kill *you!*" Sin said as he pointed the Mac 11 at her. Don still didn't speak.

"Go get the kids. We gon' whack the whole God damn house," Sin said.

"I'll tell you where the money and the dope's at! Please don't hurt my kids!" Bianca cried.

"You don't tell them anything! Fuck these fucking

niggers!" Don yelled.

"They're talking about hurting my babies! *Fuck you!*" Bianca screamed at him.

"You heard me!" he yelled.

Shaunté felt bad for Bianca. She was so scared she was pale. They only used the kids as a threat. Sin would never harm a child or an innocent person intentionally. Then Bianca had to find out this way. Don didn't give a damn about her or their kids. He cared about the money more than anything.

Shaunté pulled back and slapped Don as hard as she could with the gun and kept hitting him.

"You ain't shit! How the fuck you gonna choose money over your family!" she yelled.

"I'm going to see you again, you bitch! I'm going to kill you too!" he said.

"I'd like to see that trick. *What you gonna do, come back from the resurrection*?" Sin asked in his bad *Scarface* imitation. "Go get the money," he said to Bianca. She got up and Shaunté followed her. Sin looked at Don then raised his mask.

"All you had to do was give my nigga, Mario, his money. All I was going to do was rob you and leave, but you had to start talking shit," Sin said.

Shaunté and Bianca came back. Shaunté was dragging a big green army bag and Bianca was dragging a medium sized box.

"This fool had 25 keys sitting back there, and that box has

money filled to the top," Shaunté said. Sin looked at Don and saw the look of fear.

"Th… Th… That's the Garza's money!" Don stuttered.

"Fuck you and the Garzas!" Shaunté shouted as she opened the box and pulled out a three inch stack and gave it to Bianca. She then took her mask off.

"You go up there and get your kids and get as far away from here as possible," she said.

Don looked like he was about to make a run for it.

"You gotta better chance with the Garzas than trying to run up outta here," Sin said. Shaunté clocked him with the gun again, knocking him out. Sin looked at Bianca.

"Go!" he said. She went upstairs with Shaunté following.

"Don't try to cross us up. We could've easily killed you and the kids. Forget everything you've seen. Me and my brother will be on the highway back to LA and you will never see us again," Shaunté said.

"This is bad karma. I should never have started messing with Don. He was best friends with my son's father. When my son's father went to jail I started seeing Don," she said.

"Yeah, girl, you got some serious issues. You better make things right with your baby's daddy," Shaunté said as they walked into one of the bedrooms.

Bianca turned the light on and Shaunté saw the sleeping boy. He was light skinned with long braids.

"Is he black?" Shaunté asked.

"His father's mom is," she said as she went to the closet and grabbed a jacket for him. She then woke him up.

"Come on, Trey. We're leaving," Bianca said. The little 6 year old boy got up and put his coat on. They all walked out, and he went to the bathroom while they went to another room and got the 2 year old girl.

Bianca went and got her purse and she and the kids went downstairs. They went through the door that led to the garage. There was a gray 1998 Land Cruiser in there. Shaunté helped Bianca get the kids in the truck.

"Girl, I'm telling you. Get you a dude who'll put you and your babies before all. When you leave here, don't come back. If the police question you, make up whatever. Just don't say the wrong thing," Shaunté said as she ejected the clip from her gun and cleared the chamber.

"Hold this," Shaunté said as she handed her the gun. She reached in and unhooked the car phone. Bianca handed her the gun back. *Your ass go to the police, your prints are on this gun, not mine,* Shaunté thought as she reloaded.

"Thank you for not…"

"Ain't no need to thank me. We don't hurt innocent people or babies," Tay said. "Now get!" Bianca hit the remote and when the garage door was up she left.

Don started coming to as Shaunté came in.
"What you wanna do with this bitch!" Shaunté asked.

"Go get the truck," Sin said as he gave her the keys. Shaunté handed him her gun before she left. Sin got up and walked over to Don and picked up a pillow.

"This is your own fault, homie," Sin said with no emotion. He put the pillow to Don's head and pushed the gun in and pulled the trigger. Don was dead on impact. When Shaunté pulled into the garage, they loaded the stuff in then left. They hit the freeway back to the "O".

When they got to Sin's, he called Rod and asked where the money counter was. When he found it he started counting. Shaunté went into the bedroom and took all her clothes off and put on one of Sin's T-shirts. She came in and started separating and binding the money. Sin counted 10 gee stacks. When they were done it came up to $850,000. Sin put Maria's $400,000 to the side. He then gave Shaunté $150,000. He kept 150,000, and put aside $100,000 to put back in Rod's stack.

"Me and the baby need more than that," she said. Sin was putting the money in his duffle bag and stopped in mid motion.

"You serious?" he asked.

Shaunté nodded.

"I went and bought a test. I have an appointment with my doctor tomorrow," she said. Sin put his arm around her and hugged her.

"That's cool. Maybe it will slow your ass down some," he said.

Sin grabbed the box with the 10 keys and dumped it into the army bag with the other 25. He then took it and hid it in the bedroom. When he came out he changed back into what he had on earlier and put his black clothes up.

"Drop me off at my mama's," he said. They went outside and Sin pulled the K5 into the garage. He then got in the Yukon and Shaunté took him to his mom's. After he hid his money he got in the SS and went to Richmond.

This shit is falling right in place, he thought as he pulled up to the gates at Sheree's. He turned his music down and called her.

"Hello!" she answered sleepily.

"Baby, I'm at the gate," he said.

"Okay," she said and hung up. When the gate opened he pulled in and went to the back and parked. He got out and went up the stairs and Sheree opened the door and he went in.

Only after the door was closed did Sin notice Sheree was naked.

"I stayed up waiting for you until 1," she said as she hugged and kissed him. She took his coat and hung it up and followed him to the bedroom.

"Niggas talking that drought shit. I was meeting these people who was suppose to have some cool prices," he said as Sheree lay down.

He got undressed and got on the bed and spread her legs and licked her left inner thigh, then the right. When he got to her pussy he didn't give it a second thought. He gave Sheree about 15 minutes of outstanding head. She came twice before she moved away and rolled him on his back. Sheree sucked his dick real good. Sin didn't want to bust one in her mouth, he wanted some pussy. He pushed her head away and he got up and lay her on her back. Sheree opened her legs long enough for him to get in then closed them. Sin rode her for 45 minutes. He nutted and Sheree came soon after.

Chapter Nine

Back On the Grind

Sin woke up the next morning and Sheree was gone. He saw the note on the pillow that read:

> "*Baby, I had to go to court for a ticket. I got you some keys made and a gate control. Your breakfast is in the microwave. Call me sometime today.*"

Sin picked his phone up and called Maria.

"Hello!" she answered. Sin could tell she was asleep.

"Hey, that little thing is handled and I'm on my way out there," he said.

"Okay," she mumbled and hung up.

Sin got up and got in the shower. When he got out he put on some tan Sean John shorts, a wife beater, a short sleeved Burberry button up shirt which he left unbuttoned, white Nike ankle socks, and some tan and white Air Max. He put on the rope, ring, Rolex, and bracelet and went and brushed his teeth. He ate and left. He called Shaunté and told her to meet him at the house.

When Sin turned the corner on his block he saw Shaunté's Lexus. He pulled up and got out.

"I got some shit to do. If anyone calls me, I'll call you and give you their numbers. Don't go see nobody by yourself," he said as he opened the front door and went in. He went in the bedroom and got 10 keys and put them in a box and carried them to the Lexus.

"What time you coming back?" she asked.

"Before 8," Sin said and kissed her. He got in the SS and rode off.

Sin got on the freeway and lit his blunt. He pushed the remote and Jay Z came on bumping hard. As soon as Sin got over the Altamont he turned the A/C on full blast. When he finally got to Lodi he went straight to Maria's. He parked behind the black Expedition and went to the door and rang the bell. A few seconds later Maria was at the door.

"Who's there?" she asked.

"Sin!" he answered.

Maria opened the door wearing a pink half shirt that didn't cover the lower part of her titties, and a pink thong. Her wide hips, sexy thighs, and the imprint of her coochie had Sin's mouth watering. She closed and locked the door and turned and went towards her room. Her ass looked as if it was clapping as she walked. Sin licked his lips as he followed her.

Sin handed her the bag of money and she just threw it on the floor and crawled back in the bed.

"Lay down with me," she said. He took his shoes, shirt and wife beater off and lay down.

"I feel like shit," she said as she pulled him so close his

face was in the titties.

"You drank too much last night," he said as he put his hand on her butt and pulled her closer. Maria put her leg over him.

"I got another problem I need help with. We're having major problems with the fuckin Colombians. It's so bad, I'm moving to the Bay Area next week," she said as she rubbed Sin's head. "I can get use to this cuddling with you stuff."

"So what kind of problems you having with these cats?" he asked as he rubbed her butt.

"They tried to rob me. They've killed some of our people, and they followed me one night that I know of. I'm not supposed to tell anyone this. When my brother was out, he had all of Northern Cali on lock, from Eureka to Bakersfield. I have it now, or what's left since the Colombians came. They don't know that I'm in charge

Sin looked her in her eyes and saw that she was genuinely scared. "Baby, don't tell nobody what you told me. This is a dog eat dog game. Shit, for all you know, I could be a muthafucka that'll kill you for the type of cash you playing with," he said.

"I know this sounds crazy but I trust and have faith in you. I know I've only known you all of two days, but I know you won't cross me and you'll have my back," she said.

This could be my ticket outta the game. All I gotta do is stay cool and keep it real with these folks, Sin thought.

"Don't think because you a dime and you about to give me some pussy that I'm doing this. I'm doing it because *your brother's* a good dude, and I'm trying to get some real money," he said.

"Hold on muthafucka! Who said I was giving you some pussy?" she asked with a fake attitude. Sin rubbed his finger down the crack of her ass and stroked her pussy from the back through her panties.

"You ain't going to give me none?" he asked.

"Nope, because you got me twisted. I ain't gotta use my looks or my pussy to get what I want," she said seriously.

"You mad at me?" he asked as he lifted the half shirt and licked her left nipple.

"No," she whispered.

Sin licked the right nipple and Maria moved back against his hand. She reached down and unbuttoned his shorts and stuck her hand in his boxers and played with his dick.

"Don't get yourself worked up, because we ain't fixing to fuck," she said. Just then Sin's phone rang.

"What's up?" he answered.

"Sin, what thangs lookin like?" Bo asked.

"I'm outta town. Don't leave your phone. I'll have somebody holla at you."

"I want to spend my chips on one and get fronted one."

"When she come, give her 17-5 and owe me 17-5," Sin

said and hung up. He called Shaunté's mobile.

"What's up, daddy?" she answered.

"Boo, my boy want to get two whole ones. He's going to give you 17-5. The other 17-5's on me."

"Do I gotta count his money?" she asked.

"That's up to you," he said as he gave her Bo's number and hung up.

Maria rolled over on top of Sin and straddled him.

"Take these shorts off," she said as she raised up. He did and she lay down on him. Sin's dick was making a tent in his boxers and Maria had her panty clad pussy right up against it. The next thing he knew, Maria was sleep. *Yeah I'm going have your ass begging for some dick sooner or later*, he thought.

Chapter Ten

Him, Her, And...Her.

Within 3 weeks of hooking up with Maria, Sin was sitting on $750.000. The drought was at its height. Keys were going for as much as $25,000 and $30,000 out of state. The only people who had dope in the town were The Circle.

Sin put Shaunté, Déja, Lisa, and Juanda on the Colombians in Stockton. All they were suppose to do was set them up, but as soon as Juanda went back to Seattle with four keys, Shaunté and Déja killed the five main guys. The head man, Pedro Garza, was not around and he only knew the girls as Sharon, Dana, Juanita, and Alissa, all from Fresno.

Sin and Sheree's relationship was going perfect. He knew Sheree was gone on him. His relationship with Shaunté was all bad. He faked on Tracy in Reno, and she was very salty about it. He and Maria still hadn't had sex and that was only because she was in Arizona at her dying grandmother's bedside.

Sin was at his house getting ready for the party Rod and June were throwing him at the Omni Club. He looked in the mirror and was pleased with what he saw. He was wearing a cream colored three button Armani suit, a white shirt with platinum cuff links, and cream gator boots. He put on the 3 carat diamond pinky rings, the Rolex, and the thick platinum iced out link bracelet. He stuck the gold silk handkerchief in the top pocket, then put on the two and a half carat earrings.

Sin's phone rang.

"Hello!" he answered as he sprayed on some Ferragamo.

"Hey!" Maria said.

"What's up, baby?" he asked.

"I just wanted to tell you to have fun tonight, and I bought your birthday gift," she said.

"I ain't gon' have too much fun without you. You a'ight?" he asked.

"My granny passed at 4:40 this afternoon," she said.

"Aw, baby I'm sorry to hear that. I would come right now but these niggas throwing me a party. I'll tell you what though. I'll be on the red eye," Sin said.

"Thanks, baby. I'm going to let you get to your party. Have fun and don't wind up between nobody sheets. You're going to need *all* your strength," she said and blew a kiss through the phone before hanging up.

Sin grabbed the gold, felt Fedora with the beige feather, and the clear lens Armani glasses and put them on. He grabbed his 2 way, gun, keys, and phone and walked out.

He saw the chameleon green 99 Navigator sitting there and smiled. It was a gift to himself. The truck had black leather interior, wood grain dash, inside door panels, steering wheel, and green tints. It looked black from some angles, forest green from others, and it looked wet. Sin had the dude at the paint shop put six coats of wet gloss over it. Once he threw the beat in and the dubs on he had ended up spending $75,000. He got in and started it and pulled off.

When Sin was away from his neighborhood he picked up

the remote and pushed six. KRS-1's classic, *Loves Gonna Get You,* came on knocking. The six 15 inch EV woofers had the windows on the houses shaking. He sparked the blunt as he hit the freeway. *I'm almost where I need to be. Another six months and it's a wrap,* he thought.

The clock on the dash read 9:30. He pulled out his phone and called this chick named Monique he was getting at in Atlanta before he caught the case.

"Hello!" she answered. Sin heard music in the background and figured she was at a club.

"What's up, Georgia Peach?" he asked.

"Sin?"

"How you know?"

"Nobody else calls me that. I went up to the prison to see you and they said you were gone. Are you out?"

"Yeah, I been out about three months."

"And you just calling me?" she asked.

"You know what your situation was when we first stopped communicating. You moved in with your baby daddy and started doing his program and not your own."

"Kevin takes care of us," she said.

"He was sure taking care of you in that restaurant the night I met you. Anyway I was just calling out there to see if your situation changed. I'll holla at you," he said and hung up.

When Sin got to the Omni, he parked in a reserved space. He got out and passed by security with a nod. He spoke to a few people he knew and went to the VIP section and sat down with June and Rod. Tay walked up wearing a short gray dress and some gray four inch spike heeled shoes.

"Happy birthday, Daddy!" she said and handed Sin a box. He opened it and inside was a platinum and diamond link chain with a diamond and platinum skull and crossbones, which is the Mad Circle symbol. He looked up at her to say thank you and she kissed him on the lips. His luck couldn't be any worse. As he was gently pushing her away, Sheree walked up.

"What the fuck!" she yelled.

"Baby, it ain't like that," Sin said as he stood up.

"Baby my muthafuckin ass, nigga. Fuck you!" she yelled as she turned to leave. Sin grabbed her arm.

"Nigga, let me the fuck go! You told me you loved me this morning, now I see you kissing this bitch! Play with her not me!" she screamed. Sin jerked her closer to him.

"You muthafuckin scream on me again it's going to be big problems up in this bitch! Now I told you it wasn't like that. She kissed *me* on the mouth. I thought she was about to kiss me on the cheek," Sin said.

"You let her! And about the threat of their being a problem, *I* ain't scared of you. Come to Richmond and get your stuff," she said as she snatched her arm away.

Sin felt like slapping her for causing a scene at his party. "Fuck it! Lets go now," he said. He told Rod and June he'd be back and they left. When they got outside, Sheree started walking towards the SS.

"Leave my shit there," he said as he got in the Navigator. When Sheree got in he pulled off. They didn't say anything to each other the whole ride. Sheree had tears in her eyes when they pulled up at her house. When they got in the house, Sheree went and locked herself in the bathroom. Sin got all his stuff and put it in the truck. He then came back in and took Sheree's keys off his ring. He knocked on the bathroom door.

"Sin, just leave," she said.

"Open the door before I boot it off the hinges," he said.

She opened the door and he stepped in.

"We could've really made this thing work, but your being insecure in our relationship fucked it up."

"I know what I seen. Man, I showed you I loved you. Sin. You didn't have to do me like that. You made me look stupid!" she cried.

"What you saw was my ex give me a gift and kiss *me*, and me pushing her away. You talk about loving me, but you don't trust or have faith in me. That's not love, baby," he said as he handed her the keys. She walked out and got the keys to the SS out of her purse. Sin took them and left.

Sin sat outside Sheree's apartment for about 15 minutes, smoking a blunt. When his phone rang it was Shaunté trying to see when he was coming back. He told her he was on his way. When Sin started his truck he looked up at Sheree's window. She was standing at the sliding glass doors looking down at him. He put the truck in gear and left.

Damn, why do I feel like I'm making a mistake? Sheree said to herself. She walked over to the house phone and picked it up and called Sin. He didn't answer so she left a voice message.

Sin looked at the caller ID when his phone rang. He saw Sheree's number and threw the phone on the passenger seat. When he finally got back to the club he was in a better mood. He picked his phone up and called Southwest Airlines and made flight arrangements.

He got out of the truck and went back into the club. He saw Juanda when he was on his way to the VIP. Every dude in the club was hawking her. Sin hugged her and grabbed a handful of ass.

"Did Shuanda come with you?" he asked.

"No, she wasn't feeling good," she said. Sin knew she was lying.

"So what you get me for my birthday?" he asked.

"What you want?" she asked suggestively.

"To do it live and uncut," he said.

"With who?" she asked. Sin saw Shaunté sitting at the table and nodded her way. Juanda turned and saw Shaunté.

"Yeah, I'm with that," she said.

"Don't go too far and stay away from these suckas," he said as he popped her on the ass. She giggled and walked away.

Sin walked over to the table and sat down.

"What happened?" Shaunté asked.

"We ain't fuckin around no more," he said.

"Fuck that smart mouth bitch. That bitch don't know how we do it if she flashed on that she was insecure with ya'lls' relationship," Shaunté said. Sin laughed. It was a trip how much he and Tay thought alike.

"So what? You ready to get back on my team?" he asked.

"Nigga, I'm ready to *be* the team," she said. They sat and got their drink on.

At 1:30 Sin was ready to go. He looked for Shaunté and saw she and Juanda dancing. She looked at him and he nodded for the door and she nodded back.

"I'm gone," he said to June and Rod. He pulled his phone out and called Maria and told her he would be arriving at 8:30 in the morning. He stopped at a table where Terell sat, getting at this 25 year old chick with an okay face, but a stripper's body.

"Tee, take the SS to your house for me," he said as he handed him the keys and left. June caught him outside.

"Sin, call me in the morning. I gotta holla at you."

"A'ight," Sin said as he, Juanda, and Tay left.

"I told Lisa to take my car," Tay said as she walked toward the SS.

"Nah, baby. We in this," he said as he handed her the keys.

"Whose is this?" she asked.

"My gift to me," he said as he opened her door and she got in.

Sin opened the back door and Juanda got in, and he got in behind her.

"What you doing?" Shaunté asked.

"You remember what I asked for?"

"Yeah, and I said *I* would. I didn't say *you* could," she said faking anger.

"Shaunté, just let me give him a little something for his birthday," Juanda asked. Shaunté looked at Sin and smiled.

"Be glad it's your birthday," she said and started the truck and pulled off. Juanda unzipped Sin's pants and pulled his dick out and started sucking.

"Hit Uptown Liquors," he moaned as he lifted Juanda's leg over the front seat. He started fingering her naked, hairless pussy. Shaunté looked at him through the rearview mirror.

"You like that, daddy?" she asked.

"It's cool," he said.

"Is she better than me?"

"She's pretty good, but no ones better than you," he said.

When they were pulling up to the store, Sin and Juanda straightened up.

"Ya'll want something from in here?" he asked.

"I'm going in with you," Shaunté said.

"Me too," Juanda said. They all got out and there were like five dudes standing around. Sin took both the girls' hands and walked past the guys and went in the store. Shaunté went and grabbed some whipped cream. Juanda came up to her.

"You think we should tell him we already got down?" she asked.

"Nah, we'll show him the tape tomorrow," Tay said as she rubbed Juanda's soft ass.

Sin looked at the liquor selection. "Give me some Magnums, some Philly's, and two bottles of XO," he said as Shaunté walked up.

"$247.56," the Arab said as he stared at Shaunté.

"Man, what the fuck you lookin at?" Sin asked as he pulled a meatloaf out his pocked and slammed $300 on the counter. The Arab took the money and gave him his change. They all walked out.

"Man, I'm trying to do it like that!" one of the young dudes said.

"Aw man, you know, I dos what I do," Sin said as he

kissed Tay, then Juanda. He then looked at Juanda and nodded toward Shaunté. Juanda tongued Shaunté down.

"Daaaaamm!" they all said.

"How can I be down?" one of them said.

"You can't," Shaunté said.

Sin knew the young cats were out there getting money, and by the looks of them, they were hungry and weren't eating right. They were looking major dusty.

"Give me a cigarette, baby," he said to Juanda. She opened the door to the truck and leaned in to get her purse and her dress rose up in the back almost giving up a shot of the ass. Sin lifted it up and the young dudes' eyes bugged out.

"Baby, stooooop!" she whined and hit his hand. She gave him a cigarette and he lit it. He looked at the youngster.

"Ya'll niggas wanna get some real money?" he asked.

"What you talking about?" one of them asked.

"I'm talking about fronting you niggas a quarter cake. All I want is $4,500 back. Ain't no reason for ya'll to be out here taking these risk and ain't getting shit. You cats need to eat just like everybody else."

"Big Homie, you look like you eating good. Yeah we with it," one of them said.

"Niggas gotta get they money first. The broads gonna be there when they recognize what type of muthafucka you are. I knocked my lil' rider right here the same day I got out the pen. She get down as hard ad I do," he said and kissed Tay on her forehead. "Give these niggas your number," he said to Shaunté. She wrote her number down and gave it to the young cat.

"You know we on that Mad Circle time," she said.

"That's cool," the other one said.

"Call tomorrow," Sin said as he got in on the passenger side. Shaunté drove off.

"You on a straight money mission. Here we are about to go have a freak session and you're trying to make money," Shaunté said.

"Tay, hurry up! I'm hot!" Juanda said.

When they pulled up at Shaunté's house they all got out.

"I need to go take a shower. I'm hella sweaty from dancing all night," Juanda said.

"Me too," Tay said as they went towards the bedroom. Sin lay his .45 on the coffee table then sat down and rolled a blunt. He dialed his voice mail and listened to the message from Sheree.

"Sin, I'm hella emotional right now. Will you please come over tomorrow so we can talk? Have a happy birthday, and stay away from that bitch!" she said and hung up. Sin stripped to his boxers and sat on the sofa.

He saw the camcorder sitting on the entertainment center. *Oh it's on!* he thought as he got up. He took the tape that was in it out and put a fresh one in and turned it on. Sin pointed the camera at his face.

"This that nigga, Sin. It's my birthday, and this is how I'm living!" he said and blew blunt smoke into the lens. He then walked to the bathroom in the hall and didn't hear anything. He went to Tay's bedroom and he heard the shower going in the master bathroom. Sin opened the door and walked in. He saw Tay and Juanda's silhouettes.

"Open the door," he said. Shaunté opened the stained glass door, and as soon as she and Juanda saw the camera they went into performance mode. Shaunté put her arms around Juanda's waist and pulled her in close and kissed her. Juanda kissed down Shaunté's neck, and when she got to her titties she locked on her nipple.

"Baby, the only thing missing is you. Come get in," Shaunté said. Sin put the camcorder down and took his boxers off and got in behind Shaunté.

"Unh Unh, baby. This is for you," Shaunté said as she turned around and went to her knees. She started sucking Sin's dick while she fingered Juanda's pussy. Juanda started kissing Sin.

"I can't get loose in here. Lets go get in the bed," Tay said.

They all showered then went to the bedroom. Sin lay down and Juanda started sucking his dick again. Shaunté loved watching Juanda service Sin. As she set the camera up she felt her nipples hardening more. She sat in the chair and rubbed her pussy with one hand and brought her titty to her mouth with the other one. She licked her nipple and Sin sat there watching.

Shaunté threw her leg over the side of the chair and started moaning.

Sin started nutting and Juanda tried to swallow it all. She had nut coming out the corners of her mouth and dripping down her chin and onto her titties. Shaunté got up and pulled Sin off the bed.

"Daddy, sit in the chair," she said and got on the bed and started licking the cum off of Juanda's chin and titties. Juanda lay down and Shaunté grabbed her legs and held them wide open. She then went down on Juanda like she'd been doing it forever.

"Ooh yes, baby! Right there!" Juanda moaned. Sin was so turned on right then, and loved Shaunté even more.

"You like that, Juanda?" he asked.

"Yes, I'm about to cum!" she screamed. Sin grabbed the camera and got a close up of Tay doing her thing She started going faster as Juanda came. Sin got up and sat back in the chair. He had a perfect view of Shaunté's pussy from the back.

"Lil' mama, play with yourself," he said. Shaunté reached under herself and started fingering her pussy with her index finger and rubbing her asshole with her middle finger. Sin felt himself getting hard again. Tay lay down and Sin got a close up. Juanda turned her until she was on her hands and knees and started licking her pussy and her ass. Juanda's pussy was there in view so Sin slid into her. Sin fucked Juanda hard and she started bucking back against him.

They all went at it for another two hours and then Sin got up and went and got in the shower. Shaunté came in a few minutes later. They both showered and got out. Juanda was knocked out when they came out of the bathroom. Sin got dressed.

"Put something on and come on. I'm leaving you 10 keys. When you get down to the last two, cook them and sell fat ass rocks on Bromly, 27th and 48th ," he said. Shaunté put on a leather coat and nothing else.

"How long you gonna be gone?" she asked.

"Probably until Tuesday. Call me as soon as you run out and I'll have my hook up drop something off to you," he said as he picked up his keys. They locked up and got in the Navigator and smashed off.

When they got to Sin's house, he took all his stuff from Sheree's in and packed a suitcase and over night bag, then changed clothes. They then left for the airport.

"Did you enjoy your freak show?" he asked. She leaned over and kissed him while he kept his eyes on the road.

"That shit was off the chain! I'm going back and get some more after I drop you off. Sin, what was you doing, trying to test me or something?" she asked.

"I'm trying to make you into the perfect woman for me. You'll be perfect once you have my little one," he said as he rubbed between her legs.

"I'm about to be on Juanda's head all weekend," she said as they pulled into the airport. Sin leaned over and kissed her.

"Let Terell ride the SS tomorrow then lock it up. You know where the dope's at, and I'll call you later on," he said as they got out. He got his stuff out of the back and walked Tay around to the driver side. She got in and he kissed her again.

"Don't forget the baby!" she said. Sin kissed her stomach and then hurried into the airport. He boarded his flight, put his earphones on and listened to Mary J. Blige and went to sleep.

Chapter Eleven

Caught Up!!!

It was 7:30 A.M. when the Oakland Police drug task force, along with Berkeley's task force, finished their plan. They were about to run into Bo Andrews' house. Bo was getting big money now that he was fucking with Sin and his name was ringing. Bo went about getting money to the point he would seriously hurt anyone in his eight-man crew if they came up even $20 short. He went even harder on the crack heads. Rumor had it there was a drunk and a smoker who accidentally gave him a 10 instead of a $20 bill and Bo threw gasoline on him and set him on fire.

The black officer, known as Tony Johnson, was leading the raid. On his side was his partner, Mike Perez.

"She's leaving," he said.

"Unit One, the girl and the kid are leaving. The second she passes your position we're going in," Perez said into the Nextel phone.

"Unit One to command. She passed me and crossed Ashby," the reply came back over the phone.

"All units move in!" Perez yelled into his phone. Johnson jumped out of the van and ran up the stairs. Five other officers ran around the house. All of them had on blue or black jackets with either Oakland Police or Berkeley Police stenciled in gold letters, bulletproof vests, and guns drawn.

Johnson nodded at Perez, and then stood back and kicked

the door off the hinges. They ran in checking the rooms and proceeded to the back. When they came in the bedroom, Bo was sitting there in his boxers reaching for his pants.

"ON THE FUCKIN FLOOR, ASSHOLE!" Perez yelled. Bo did as told and Johnson cuffed him and sat him on the bed.

"Tell us where the dope's at or we're going to tear your girl's house up," Johnson said.

"Hold on, man. Can I talk to ya'll?" Bo asked.

"Talk," Perez said.

"Privately," he said. Johnson looked at the other cops and nodded to the door. When they were gone Bo sighed.

"Man, what ya'll on me for? I'm a small fry in this shit," he said. Bo saw he wasn't getting anywhere. "I'll give you my connect if you let me go."

"Bo, we got you for possessing and distributing base cocaine, and attempted murder. Give us a murder and your connect and we'll let you go," Johnson said.

"My connection's name is Sin Michaels. He just recently got out of prison in Georgia. His brother is Erick Michaels, and his cousin's Rodney Coleman. They're part of the Mad Circle. He messes with a chick named Shaunté. She was the one that downed them dudes, Alonzo and Jeff, at Roscoe's a few months ago and Sin was there. Man, since this drought started, Sin's kept a constant supply of dope and he's only charging 17-5. Cat's from all over the Bay Area been coming out here buying dope from him. I can hand Sin to ya'll on a silver platter," Bo said.

Just then, another officer came in carrying 3 keys. "We found this in the bathroom closet," he said.

Johnson wanted to bust Bo badly, but he wanted to get the person who committed those murders and bust the dude with all the dope. This could be he and Perez's tickets to the FBI.

"Uncuff him," he said to Perez. When that was done, Johnson sat in a chair across from Bo.

"You working for us now. When we're ready, we'll call you. Don't think about fuckin us over, Andrews. I promise I'll put the word in the street that you're a rat, and I will make sure the Feds pick up this dope case. I'll also get the D.A. to file an attempted murder with special circumstances charges against you," Johnson said as he picked up Bo's cell phone and looked at the number. He then programmed it into his phone and handed Bo a card.

"Get as close to this dude, Michaels, as you can," Perez said as he threw the 3 keys on the bed. He and Johnson and the rest of the officers then left.

Fuck! What am I doing to do? Shit, I ain't got no choice. It's either me doing life or this nigga doing life. Fuck that nigga, and the rest of the Mad Circle, Bo thought.

Chapter Twelve

Arizona Heat

When Sin got off the plane, Maria was there waiting for him.

"Hey, lil' mama!" he said. She walked up to him and hugged him and kissed him on the lips.

"Thank you for coming," she said. They walked out the airport and got into a gray Lexus RX-470 truck.

"So how was the party last night?" she asked.

"It was a'ight. I preferred to be with you though," he said.

"Don't worry. We'll celebrate your birthday tonight," she said. Maria was wearing a short yellow dress and white sandals. She looked as if she was a couple of shades darker.

"So when's the funeral?" he asked.

"Monday," she said as they pulled out.

They rode for about 20 minutes, then Maria pulled in front of a black gate. She hit the remote and the gate opened and they pulled in. They drove down a tree and grass lined road. They passed a barn then some horse stables with over 20 horses. Then they came to the small mansion.

"Damn, how many rooms are in here?" Sin asked in awe.

"There's 9 bedrooms, 6 bathrooms, and 4 guest houses. One of them is mine and Mario has one. They all have Jacuzzis.

There's a pool, and a 12 car garage. My dad bought this for my mom when they got divorced." They pulled in front of the house and got out.

"Wait until you see my mom. She's the greatest. People don't believe we're mother and daughter. She's 50, but she looks like she's 30. After 4 kids she still has a nice body. She looks like one of them video chicks," Maria said. Just then a girl came out that could be Maria's twin.

"That's my little sister, Cynthia. She's going to be moving to the Bay Area with me. Oh, I forgot to tell you I got the house in Lafayette. The realtor called me when I was on the way to get you." The girl walked up.

"Cynt, this is Sin," Maria said. Cynthia sized Sin up. *Oh yeah, he's fine,* she said to herself.

"You gotta a little brother that looks like you?" she asked.

"I gotta a little brother, but he don't look like me," Sin said. They went in the house and Sin looked around at all the marble, crystal, the paintings, and all the priceless vases.

"Mama!" Maria yelled.

Sin saw a tan-colored woman, who favored Maria and Cynthia come to the top of the grand staircase. She was wearing a loose fitting shirt and loose fitting jeans, but Sin could tell she had body.

"Hold on! You black?" he asked.

"I was the last time I checked," she said as she came down the stairs. They all laughed. "I'm Janine," she said.

"I'm Sin."

"I bet you are. So I take it he's staying in the guest house with you?" she asked Maria.

"For sure. I wouldn't leave him in here with you and your hot ass daughter!" Maria joked.

"You got nerve! You've served more coochie than McDonald's served burgers," Cynthia joked.

"Come on, Sin before these people turn you against me," Maria said and laughed.

She showed Sin around the house then they went back to the car and got his stuff.

"It's hot as hell out here."

"I'll take you to the mall so you can get some shorts and stuff," she said as they walked to her house. When they got inside the house looked like a plushed out hotel suite.

"So what do you want to do?" Maria asked.

"Rest. I'm hella tired."

"Go ahead. I'll have Leena make you something to eat," she said. Sin kicked his shoes off and lay down on the soft, king-sized bed and was out within minutes.

When Maria came back in she put the Chicken cheese Tacos and Strawberry soda on the nightstand and gently shook Sin awake.

"Baby, eat," she whispered. Sin sat up and devoured the food.

After he finished eating, she told him to get undressed. He got up and got undressed and got in the bed. Maria stepped out of her dress and all that remained was her panties. She lay in Sin's arms and scooted back until her soft ass was pressed against him. Sin got hard instantly. He knew that was what she hoped to accomplish, but Shaunté and Juanda had worn him out. Later on though, he was going to serve her.

Sin woke up at 3:00 and Maria was gone. He washed up and got dressed and went to the main house. When he walked in the kitchen Janine and the housekeeper, Leena, were cooking.

"Oh, you're up. Maria took Cynthia to take her driver's test. You want to see the property?" she asked.

"Yeah, for sure," he said. She took her apron off and walked out with Sin following with his eyes glued to her ass. They got into a golf cart and she showed him her estate. They stopped by the stables.

"Which one of those horses do you like?" Janine asked. Sin looked at all of them then looked back at the burnt orange one with the gold mane and tail.

"I like that one. He looks fast," he said and pointed.

"Why do you think that?"

"Look at his chest muscles, and the muscles in his legs," he said.

"Your assumption was right on the mark, but you were

wrong about one thing. It's a girl, not a boy. She's yours. What're you gonna name her?" she asked.

"Sunset."

"John, I've given Simian the orange mare, and he named her Sunset. I want her in the pen with Midnight. Then if you would, please saddle her and Beauty," she said.

"Yes, ma'am," he said.

"I'll be back," Janine said.

Sin got out of the cart and she drove off. Once John saddled the horses Sin walked up to Sunset and attempted to get on her and she moved away.

"Easy girl," he said. He tried again and she moved again. "You about to piss me off!" John sat on the fence and laughed. Sin tried again and she didn't move.

"See, that wasn't ha…" He didn't finish his sentence. Sunset bucked him off, and Sin landed in the dirt.

"You okay?" John asked. Sunset nudged him with her nose. Sin couldn't help but laugh as he got up and brushed himself off.

"You like to play hard to get, huh, pretty lady. I think I'll call you Hard to Get, or better yet Heart Breaker. I know one thing though, you buck me again they gon' call your ass dog food!" Sin said.

He got back on her and she submitted. He rode her from one end of the pen to the other.

"John, is there anything sticking out of the ground over there?" Sin asked as he pointed to the 100-yard stretch of grass.

"No it's clear," he said. Sin walked Heart Breaker to the stretch of grass and tapped her sides and she took off. *Damn, she's fast!* he thought. When he got to the end of the stretch he turned her around and ran her back.

When he stopped, John was standing on the ground. "I didn't know she was that fast. We should breed her with Mario's horse, Midnight," he said.

"I'm only going to be here for a few days. Will you run her from time to time for me?" he asked as he pulled a $100 bill out his pocket.

"There's no need for that. I would be honored to take care of her," John said.

"You got kids?" Sin asked.

"Yes," he said.

Sin grabbed John's hand and put the $100 bill in it. "Father's Day is Sunday. Happy Father's Day," he said.

John thought about it and smiled. "Since you put it like that, thank you!" Just then Janine pulled up.

"Are you ready?" she asked as she got out the cart. She was wearing a wife beater, no bra, some skin tight, well worn light blue Levi's that had holes in the knee's and thighs just below her butt, and black cowboy boots. Janine was built just like Maria. The only difference was Maria had a flat stomach from working out and Janine had a little loose skin around her stomach, bigger titties, wider hips, and a bigger ass.

Deezam, this lady got body! Sin thought. He helped her up on her horse and walked over to his and got on and they rode off. Sin watched Janine's titties bouncing up and down. *I gotta stop this shit!* They rode to the other side of the property to some trees. Janine pulled a joint out her pocket.

"Do you smoke?" she asked.

"Sometimes. This Arizona heat is killing me!" Sin said as he got off Heart Breaker and took his shirt off.

Nice! Janine thought. She lit the weed hit it a few times and passed it. Sin hit it and frowned.

"Nah, Janine. This here ain't the one. I got something that will knock your boots off," he said as he got back on his horse. As they rode back, Sin imagined himself as being Janine's saddle and started getting hard. The way she rode left no doubt in his mind that she could ride a dick.

When they got to Maria's, Sin ran in and got two half ounces of weed, two Garcia Vega's and two bottles of Evian. He came back out and they rode back to the trees. They got off their horse and let them graze on the grass. They sat under a shade tree and Sin stripped the Vega's of tobacco and broke a nice size bud down. Janine picked the bag of weed up.

"How much is this?" she asked.

"A half ounce."

"No, how much does it cost?" she asked.

"A whole ounce is $400," he said.

"I pay $800 for an ounce of the stuff I get," she said.

"You getting robbed," he said as he handed her a blunt.

"Cynthia smokes these. She thinks I don't know it though," she said as she sparked up.

Janine inhaled the blunt and started coughing. She passed Sin the weed and he hit it.

"That's some good shit," Janine said and started giggling. Sin gave her a nice size bud for herself and they sat and talked for a little while.

"It is hotter than hell out here," she said and cracked open the frosty bottle of water. She took a sip then poured some down the back of her wife beater. "Whew! That felt good."

"Damn! I wanna hit the pool, but I didn't bring any shorts."

"Swim in your underwear. It's okay," Janine said. Sin noticed her nipples poking through the material of her wife beater.

"I think I'll do that," he said as he stood and helped her up. When she stood she was so close that her titties touched his chest.

"Excuse me," he said. She smiled at him.

"No excuse necessary," she said as she switched her big sexy ass over to her horse.

She don't know, she gon' fuck around and get what she asking for. Nah, never would I fuck off the connection with Mario and Maria. Its way too much loot involved, Sin thought as he got on his horse.

They rode back to the stables and left the horses with John. Janine then dropped Sin off.

"I'll see you at the pool," she said and drove off in the golf cart.

Sin went in the house and grabbed a towel and a bottle of water. His phone rang. He looked at the caller ID and saw who it was.

"What up, Bo?" he asked.

"I need to see you, Dawg."

"I'm on the under for a couple of days, but I'll have somebody holla at you. Stay by the phone," Sin said and hung up. He called Shaunté.

"What's up, baby?" she asked.

"Call that nigga, Bo," Sin said and gave her the number. "Everything cool?" he asked.

"Yeah, it's cool."

"Alright. I'll holla at you later on," he said and hung up.

Sin picked up another water and went out to the pool. As he was taking his pants off he noticed Janine boldly staring at him from her bedroom terrace.

Why is she playing with me? he asked himself as he dived in. When he came up, she was gone. He heard some loud music coming. He swam for a little while, then Maria came into the pool area and Sin swam over to her.

"Did you have a good rest?" she asked.

"Yeah, but I missed you," he said as he looked up the front of her dress.

"I'm fixing to go change so I can jump in."

"I'm the one wanting to jump in," he flirted.

"Oh, believe you will!" she said as she switched off.

Sin got out of the pool and sat in the lounge chair. Cynthia came in the pool area wearing a neon green thong swimsuit.

"Girl, you gon' catch a dude a case," Sin said.

"I turn 18 next month so I'm legal," she said. Sin just shook his head.

"I got my license!" she said excitedly.

"So what you gon' get?" he asked.

"My dad want's me to get a little more driving experience so I'll probably get an Acura for now. Call your brother," she asked as she handed him the phone. Sin called Terell.

"Hello!" he answered.

"What's up?" Sin asked.

"Nothing but his loot, man," Terell said.

"I got a little cutie that want to meet you," Sin said.

"What she look like? Is she fine?"

"She's *like* that. She's Puerto Rican and Black, about 5'7", 130 pounds, long ass black hair and green eyes."

"She got body?" Terell asked as he served a crack head.

"Yeah."

"Big titties?"

Sin looked at Cynthia's chest. "Yeah, they hella big," he said.

"34DD," Cynthia bragged.

"How big?"

"About as big as Déja's."

"Damn! What about her ass?" he asked.

"Turn around," Sin said. Cynthia did and Sin sighed.

"Just a little smaller than Déja's."

"How old is she?" Terell asked.

Sin handed Cynthia the phone. "Hello!" she answered.

"What's up, lil' mama?"

"Nothing. What's up with you?"

"Nothing. My brother tells me you a top notch."

"I'm alright."

"Baby, my brother only fools with beauties, and if he said you was fine then I gotta run with that."

Maria came out in a white thong swimsuit carrying their phones and a towel. She handed Sin his phone. He looked at the phone and saw Sheree's number.

"What's up?" he asked clearly irritated.

"Damn, that's how you greet me now?" she asked angrily.

"You said what you had to say last night, ain't shit else to talk about."

"Who answered your phone?"

"Why?"

"Look, Sin. I saw what I saw. I wanna come talk to you."

"I'm in Arizona, and I won't be back until next week, and I really ain't trying to talk anyway. I gotta go," he said and hung up.

"Poor baby!" Maria said and dove in. Sin dove in and swam to her. He got her in the corner and reached up to hold on to the sides. Maria wrapped her legs around him and leaned back against the wall.

"I like this suit," he said.

"You just like my fat butt," she said.

"You need to cut that shit out. You know your butt is sexy as hell."

Maria put her arms around Sin's neck. "What do you want from me, besides sex?" she asked seriously.

"Baby, I want you. What you got don't mean shit to me. I got the tools to get it for myself," he said. Maria kissed him. Sin slid his tongue in her mouth.

"Baby, I'm spoiled, and I like getting my way," she said.

"So am I, and I want it my way."

"What if our ways are different?"

"Then I'm going to have to *make* it my way," he said as he held the cement with one hand and her ass with the other.

"We'll see about that," she said.

Maria tilted her head sideways and looked at Sin. "I really like you, Sin. If this going to be some bullshit, lets just go on ahead and have fun and go on about our business. I need a man, not a fuck buddy. I can get a fuck buddy from anywhere. I'm trying to build a long lasting relationship. Are *you* with that?" she asked.

"*No question*!" he replied. Maria kissed him again and

stuck her hand in the water and pulled his dick out and stroked it until it was hard.

"Why you playin?" he asked.

"I'm not," she said.

"Let go in the house," he said.

"If you want it, take it right here!" she whispered in his ear.

Sin sank down in the water and pulled Maria's thong off. He came up and grabbed the sides of the pool again. Maria wrapped her legs around him and he slid his dick in her and she almost screamed out.

"Baby, stop! We better go in the house before I start screaming," she said in his ear. Sin pulled out and sank back down. Maria went underwater and put her thong back on.

Janine came in the pool area wearing a white bikini top with cherries, which her titties strained to escape from, and matching low-rise short *short* shorts that her ass hung out of.

"Mama, why didn't you wear the thong that goes to that top?" Maria asked.

"I did. I just didn't want to embarrass you in front of your company," she said.

"Mama, with a body like yours you could never embarrass me. You have wider hips, a smaller waist, bigger thighs, more booty and bigger tatas than me and Cynthia. I'm proud to have a mother with a body like yours," Maria said.

"Correction. Her tatas are bigger than *yours,* not mine," Cynthia said.

Janine took the shorts off and her ass had Sin staring open mouthed.

"She's beautiful," Maria said.

"I see where you and your sister get it from," Sin said.

"She has no tan lines. On Sunday's she give all her workers the day off and she sunbathes naked."

Sin started grinning. *Tomorrow's Sunday,* he thought.

"I'm going in. It's too much ass out here for me to handle," he said.

"I'll be in there in a minute," Maria said.

Sin pulled himself out of the pool. Cynthia got bug eyed and Janine gasped in surprise then grinned. "Cynthia, turn your head!" she said.

"Yeah right!" she said as she stared. Sin followed their eyes and looked down and his dick was hanging out.

"Excuse me!" he said as he tucked himself in. He grabbed the towel and left.

When Sin got to Maria's he fired up the hot tub and got in the shower. He got out and slid into the tub. Maria came in laughing.

"You better stop flashing the goods," she said.

"That shit was an accident. I was hella embarrassed," he said. Maria stepped out of her swimsuit and got in the tub with him. She grabbed is dick and stroked it.

"I want you to give it to me like you ain't never gave it to anyone else," she said.

"Baby, I do that then we fixing to be together."

"That's what I'm talkin' 'bout."

Sin carried Maria to the bed and sexed her slowly for like an hour. Maria started screaming and talking in Spanish and Sin was loving that. When they came Sin cursed himself for not using a rubber.

"Damn, Papi! That was *good*!" she said.

"I got three speeds; Making love, and that's what we just did. Sex, and that's just both of us getting off. The best one is fucking. That's anything goes. Raw dog down and dirty *fuckin'*!" he said.

"So what's up, Papi? We fuckin' tonight?" she asked in Spanish.

"No question," he replied. They lay together for a little while longer and then got back in the shower. They lotioned each other down and got dressed. Sin put on some black silk boxers, some dark blue Fubu jeans, a white wife beater, some white and blue Air Max, and a blue wave cap. He put the 24" gold link chain with the weed leaf on his neck, the link bracelet on his right wrist, the gold nugget and diamond rings on his fingers, the Tag watch on his left wrist, and the 3 carat diamond earrings in his ears.

Maria put on a white and blue thong, dark blue DKNY jean skirt, white BeBe Baby tee which showed off her belly ring, and dark blue DKNY flip flops. She put some diamond studs in her ears, a few rings on her fingers, a rope with a cross, a small nugget bracelet, and a Cartier watch. She put her hair in a ponytail and put it in a white hair band.

"You ready, Papi?" she asked as she picked up her black Coach. Sin snatched up his phone and they went to the main house. She grabbed the keys to the green Benz S500 coupe and handed them to Sin. They went outside and got in the car and left.

When they got to the mall they went into Macy's. Sin bought six different colored and brand of jeans shorts. He bought a burgundy fit to go out in and 10 pairs of silk boxers. While he was at the counter he saw a nice green Girbaud fit.

"How much is that outfit?" he asked the saleslady.

"The jeans are $55, the jean jacket's $80, and the T-shirt's $25," she said. Sin walked over and got his sizes and put the stuff on the counter.

"That comes up to $625, sir. Will that be cash or charge?" she asked. Sin handed her the gold Visa and his ID. The lady looked at him five times before she processed the card. After Sin signed the slip they left.

They went to a few more stores and then left the mall. As they were pulling out a Black Dodge Ram almost hit them.

"Watch where the fuck you going, stupid!" the white guy driving yelled.

Sin stuck his hand out the window and flipped the dude

off. The dude slammed on his brakes. Sin got out of the car.

"Muthafucka, you trying to see me?" he asked. The white boy was attempting to get out of his car but his girl was pulling him back.

"Tommy, fuck this shit it ain't worth it," she said.

"Sin, please get back in the car," Maria said as she looked at the white boy. "Tommy?" She asked.

"What's up, Maria? This dude with you?" he asked.

"Yeah, he's my boyfriend."

"Okay, my bad."

"Why don't you come by and smoke with me?" she asked.

"A'ight" he said as he nodded to Sin and rode off.

Sin got back in the car and pulled out.

"Man, don't tell me you was fuckin with that wannabe Slim Shady/Fred Durst dress alike ass muthafucka," Sin said.

"Not even! Mario and Tommy's sister, Debbie, are really tight. Tommy's into hip hop so he dresses in what he likes. I've known him since my mom moved here. He's our neighbor. He and Cynthia went to school together. He's 3 years older than her."

When they got back to the ranch, Sin started getting his stuff out of the car. Janine came out in a short red sun dress that was fitting nicely.

"Dang, boy! You worse than these girls," she said and laughed.

"I gotta stay fitted," he said. Just then, Cynthia came out.

"Tommy's coming up," she said. Tommy pulled up in the circular drive and got out. He had on a white red and blue U of A Wildcats jersey with Sean Elliot's name and number, some light blue Girbaud shorts, a dark blue baseball cap turned backwards, and some white K-Swiss.

"Hey, playa. My bad for that," he said to Sin with his hand out.

"It's cool," Sin replied and shook his hand.

"How are you doing, Miss Janine?" he asked.

"I'm okay, sweetheart. How are your parents?" she asked.

"They're okay," he said.

"Tell them I said hello," she said as she turned and went back in the house followed by Cynthia.

"Baby, I'm going to clean up the house. Why don't you roll up one and you and Tommy smoke," she suggested.

"I'll meet you by the pool," Sin said to Tommy as he and Maria picked up his bags. They took the stuff into Maria's house and he rolled a blunt.

When Sin got to the pool, Tommy was smoking a blunt

while talking on his phone. He tried to pass Sin the blunt.

"Nah, I'm cool on that shit. Light this up," Sin said. Tommy lit the blunt and started choking.

"Man, this shit is some dynamite!" he said as he passed it. They talked for about an hour then Tommy left. Sin went in the house and he and Maria had sex again.

At 10:00, Sin and Maria were dressed and preparing to go to the club. Sin had on a pair of white Sean John pants, a white long sleeved Sean John button up, and some black Kenneth Cole shoes. He put the platinum pieces on and sprayed on some Joop. Maria was wearing a short Prada slip dress and heels, no bra, no panties. She blew her natural curls out and had her long silky mane coming down her back and chest, and she was rocking all diamond pieces.

They left and saw Cynthia standing by the Benz. "Where you going?" he asked her.

"With ya'll," she said and pulled out a fake ID. Maria went up the path to Mario's cottage and went to the closet and slid some paneling back, and there hung every gun known to man. Maria grabbed a 9mm Glock. She locked up and went and got into the car. She slid the gun in the console and Sin pulled off.

When they got to the club, it was packed and jumping. Sin's mobile rang. He saw June's number.

"What's up, Bro?" he asked.'

"Sin, I told you I needed to holla at you."

"Man, something came up. Holla at me, Bro."

"Hold on, somebody want's to talk to you," June said.

"Hello!" a female said.

"Who is this?" he asked.

"Malika," she said. Everything seemed as if it went quiet.

Malika was Sin's first love. They hooked up when they were both 14 and Sin was gone on her. They had an apartment together when they were both 15 and everything was right. Sin was making some cool money selling dope. He was only 15 sitting on 50 gees. He had a '69 convertible Cougar, a 4-door '79 Caprice classic, and he bought Malika a brand new cream '85 Maxima off the lot. He gave his 20 year old sister Jasmine the money and she went and got them a spot.

Sin knew Malika's mom, Tina, didn't like him, but she loved the way he took care of her daughter. She let them live together on the grounds that Malika went to school, kept her grades up, and she didn't get pregnant. Then after a month she got pregnant. Her mom and uncle showed up at their door one day three months later when Sin wasn't there and made her come back home. Malika's best friend, Simone's sister, Trina, accidentally let it slip out. When she and Sin talked to Malika on the phone that night they plotted on running away. Her mother came into her room and caught her packing and called her father and his mom in Louisiana.

By the time Sin got there, he saw Malika's mom, Tina, and her uncle, Theo, forcing her into a car. Her uncle Vince ran up on Sin threatening him, and they got into a fight while Theo pulled off. Sin shot her mom and uncle's houses up that night. No one knew where Malika was. Her best friend, Simone, who was June's baby mama, didn't know either. After a month Sin said fuck her. She knew how to call home and didn't. So he figured she said fuck *him.*

Sin wanted to cuss her out. Instead, he took a deep breath and composed himself.

"Hey, Malika. How you doing?" he asked.

"I'm okay. I wanna talk to you. Can I see you tonight?"

"I'm in Arizona and I'm not coming back until Tuesday."

"Sin, we have so much to talk about," she said. Sin was silent for a minute.

"Baby, we're going to dance," Maria said. Sin nodded and she and Cynthia walked off.

"Who was that?" Malika asked.

Sin couldn't hold it back any longer. "Why the fuck it take you 13 years to get in touch with me? I didn't deserve enough fucking consideration for you to call or write and say you wasn't coming back," he asked calmly. Malika knew he was mad.

"Baby, I did. I wrote you everyday at our house when they stopped watching me. I snuck off and called Simone and she told me you was in Juvenile Hall and you was messing with some bitch, so I was like fuck it. Your ass didn't wait no time to replace me."

"I didn't hear from you for a month and your ass knew

how to call home. I stayed home for damn near a month straight! You know mom's address. Why didn't you send them there?" he asked as his temper started getting out of control.

"I did, and the letters came back 'Return to Sender' and I got in trouble."

"Malika, it's been 13 years!"

"I came out to visit in '94 and found out you were in jail in Georgia. I also found out you had two kids."

"I'll call you tomorrow."

"I'll call you. I'll get your number from June," she said. Sin hung up.

Maria saw that Sin was beyond pissed. "What's wrong, baby?" she asked.

"I got a major headache. I'm taking a cab back to the house."

"I'll take you. Let me go get Cynthia and we can call it a night," she said.

"Naw, Boo. Just drop me off and come back and enjoy yourself," he said. Maria picked up her purse and they left.

When they got outside they saw Tommy sitting in a primer color convertible 1972 SS Chevelle with two white girls.

"What's up man? You got some more of that killer bud?" Tommy asked.

"Yeah, and I'll smoke some with you if you give me a ride to the house."

"For sure," he said.

Sin kissed Maria. "I'll see you when you get home. Don't be up here acting loose," he said.

"I told you, I'm yours. Trust me."

"Have fun!" he said.

She then looked in the car. "Stay away from my man!" she said to the white girls.

Sin popped her on the ass. "Get your ass on," he said. She handed him the remote to the gate.

"I'm not trying to hear that headache shit when I get home. Have my stuff ready," she said as she walked off switching. Maria had a very seductive walk. She had guys in a trance.

Sin looked at the girl in the front seat. She was blond, blue eyed, pale skinned, and had big titties. He opened the door and got in the back. The girl in the back was fine. She had black hair, blue eyes, full lips, a dark tan, and a more than ample chest. She was by far one of the cutest white girl he had even seen in person.

"This is a clean ass ol' school. What you want for it?" he asked Tommy.

"I'm about to do big things with this. I know where there's another one at. It needs paint, interior, and a top, but it does have a 454 engine with only 35,000 original miles. This old lady on Pima County road has it, and she only wants $1,500. I'll take you to see it tomorrow," he said.

Sin looked at the cutie. "What's up, baby? My name's Sin," he said.

"I'm Sandra."

"You ever dated a black guy?" he asked.

"Nothing but, ever since high school. You ever dated a white woman?" she asked.

"Yeah, in high school, and matter of fact she lived in my apartment with me during high school. I'm an equal opportunity lover. It ain't the color it's the woman," he said as he lit the blunt. He passed it to her and she hit it.

"This is some good stuff," she said as she passed it to Tommy.

Tommy hit the weed and started grinning.

"This shit is the bomb!" he said as he passed it to the other girl who, Sin found out was named Brittany.

"Was that your girl?" Sandra asked.

"Yeah. So what's up? Can I get your number?" Sin asked.
"What about your girl?" she asked.

"What about her?"

Sandra picked Sin's phone up off his lap and put her

number in the memory.

"So, when you want me to call?" he asked.

"When ever you want to," she said.

"What about at 5 in the morning?"

"I'll be in the bed sleep at that time."

"That's when I want to talk to you," he flirted.

"How you gonna call when you're already going be there?" she flirted back.

"I like you. You're hella cool. If nothing else, we can be good friends," he said as Tommy pulled up to the house. "Can you get out and give me a hug?" he asked Sandra.

"I don't see why not," she said.

They got out of the car and Sin saw how her ass was pushing out the white, low rise sweats. The only other white girl he had ever seen that had ass like that was his high school ex, Liz. He put his arms around her waist and hugged her.

"You better make sure you call me," she said.

"No doubt, Boo," he said as he pushed the button and walked through the parted gate. He pushed it again to close it and walked down the long drive.

Sin started thinking about how he and Malika met. It was 1985. He, his brother, and Marco pulled up at the carnival at Laney College in June's '86 300D Benz. They saw Simone and

Malika, and June immediately started getting at Simone. Sin stared at Malika for a full minute.

"What's up with you, baby?" he asked. Malika was fine, and her body wasn't that of a 14 year old girl, but of a 21 year old woman. Malika didn't think she was thick. In fact she had a complex about the size of her butt and chest. She thought she was fat.

"Not you, and I ain't your baby!" she said. After she said it she regretted it. *Damn, this boy's fine,* she thought. She was just about to apologize.

"Fuck you, you fat ass bitch!" Sin said.

"Nigga, I ain't fat!" she said as she walked up on him. Sin was about to knock her out, and June pulled him away.

"You better be glad you fine, or I'd knock your punk ass out!" Sin said as he walked away.

Sin was talking to a girl that went to Oakland High when he saw Malika surrounded by five dudes. *I hope they beat that bitch as, with her smart ass mouth,* he thought.

"Why don't ya'll just leave me alone!" she yelled. One of the dudes, a grown nigga that Sin knew from in the traffic named Freddie, grabbed her ass. Sin walked over to them.

"Nigga, what you touching all on my girl for?" he asked.

"Boy, you better go find you some business before you get stomped," Freddie threatened.

Sin pulled the 9mm Beretta out of his orange Fila puff

coat. "Come stomp me then, punk!" The dudes stood there spooked.

"Come here, man," Sin said to Malika. She ran over to him.

"Please don't shoot them. Just let them go," she begged.

"Nah, these niggas getting served."

"Fuck them! They ain't worth you going to jail," she said. When she said that, Sin looked around at the crowd that gathered.

"You niggas lucky. I'll see you again. Get the fuck up outta here," he said. The dudes broke and ran.

"Come on before these niggas come back up in here shooting."

From that day on, Sin and Malika started going together. Then one day after Malika was gone for some months, her mother, Tina, called Sin and told him to come over. When he showed, up she tried to seduce him. Tina had body just like Malika, and she was fine! Sin didn't bite though. Tina knew then she made a mistake sending her daughter away, but it was too late. She even told Sin that Malika had a miscarriage.

When Sin got to Maria's he heard splashing by the pool. He walked over by the gate and saw Janine swimming, naked. He looked up in the air. *Why is you testing me?* he thought. She got out of the pool and walked over to the lounge and got a towel. Janine's body was outstanding.

Sin walked away before he got into trouble. He went in the house and poured him a Henny over ice, stripped to his boxers, and started up the hot tub. He grabbed is phone and called his brother.

"What up, nigga?" June answered.

"Bro, Malika still with you?" he asked. June handed her the phone.

"Sin?"

"So how you been?" he asked.

"I've been okay. Just working hella hard. I work for J.A. Drake and Associates. I'm a junior partner," she said.

J.A. Drake and Associates was one of the biggest financial institutions in the world. Sin was impressed that Malika was a junior partner in the company.

"That's good. So how long are you going to be in Oakland?" he asked.

"I ain't going nowhere until I talk to you."

"I'll be back by Tuesday."

"I saw your little girl today. She is so cute."

"That should've been our little girl. Your mom told me you had a miscarriage."

"She told you that?" Malika asked sounding surprised.

"Yeah."

"Sin, I have never stopped loving you," she pleaded.

That was the last thing Sin was trying to hear.

"Malika, you fucked me up inside when you left. It took me years to trust a woman again. I dogged every female I was in a relationship with except my son's mama. I ain't never loved anyone the way I loved you," he said. Malika heard the word "loved" loud and clear. Meaning he *didn't* love her anymore. She decided to make him reminisce.

"You remember when we stayed at the Sixpence Inn the first time?" she asked. Sin started laughing.

"You would remember that. That was the first time I ever ate pussy," he said.

"I remember when we were at Motel 6, and you was going to quit me because I wouldn't suck your dick."

"You did it though," he said and laughed.

"No doubt! I wasn't about to let your fine ass dump me. I liked it too. That's why I did it for you every night we had our apartment. I almost had your ass crying a couple of times," she said and giggled.

"Yeah, you wasn't no joke with the head," Sin said.

"Shit, neither were you. You used to have me in a zone. Remember when your ass beat me up?" she asked.

"When you shot at me and put that hole in my Cougar," He said.

Just then Maria's phone rang. "Hold on," he said and answered it. "Hello!"

"Is Maria there?" some female with an attitude asked.

"Nah, she ain't here."

"My name is Dawn. Tell her I said I found her number in my man Greg's car, and to stay away from him!" she said. Sin hung up on her.

"Anyway, you saved my life remember?" he asked Malika.

"Yeah, that was the night Corey got killed. I had a feeling something was going to happen that night. I had to cry to keep you home. You heard from Marco?" she asked.

"Not since I been home. I took his mom 10 gees before I went to Atlanta. I only been home like three months."

"Sin, June Bug's battery's going out. I'm going to call you tomorrow about 10."

"A'ight" he said and hung up.

Sin decided to test his mackin'. He put some shorts on grabbed his drink and went out the door. When he got to the pool area Janine was in the deep end. He walked through the gate and she looked up at him and smiled.

"I thought you went out with Cynthia and Maria," she said.

"I had a headache. Are you in there naked?" he asked.

"This is how I swim every night."

"Let me get out your way," he said as he turned to leave.

"No, stay. I don't mind," she said. Sin sat at the table.

"You been teasing me all day. What's up wit' that?" Sin asked. Janine giggled.

"No I haven't," she said.

"I'm gone. You ain't keeping it real with me," he said as he stood up.

"No wait! Okay, I may have tried to tease you when we went riding," she said as she swam to the shallow end.

Janine walked out of the pool asshole naked and grabbed a towel. She walked over to the table and grabbed Sin's drink and took a sip.

"Come on. I want to show you something," she said as she slipped her feet into some Nike flip flops and started for the house. Sin's dick was harder than Chinese arithmetic. He followed her with his eyes glued to her ass. *What am I getting myself into?* he thought.

"I love my daughter more than anything in this world, but she's a slut. Maria fucked my ex boyfriend. They had an affair for more than a year. She doesn't know I know, and neither did he. I never even thought about getting even with her. He wasn't worth shit anyway. I have never looked twice at one of her *many* male friends she brought here," she said.

Janine stepped onto the first stair leading to the bedrooms

and turned and looked at Sin.

"Until I met you," she continued. She walked up the stairs and every step she took Sin could see her pussy from the back.

"Janine, I'm more than flattered, but I like Maria a lot, and I wouldn't want to mess up our relationship, or you two's relationship by following my little head," Sin said sincerely. Janine stopped in front of the double doors of her bedroom.

"Sin, I saw it. There's nothing little about that head," she said looking at his crotch.

You keep it up, I'm gon' lay your old sexy ass out, he thought.

They walked in Janine's room and it was huge. It was almost bigger than Sin's whole house.

Have a seat," she said and nodded to the bed. He did as told and she disappeared into the huge walk-in closet and came out wearing a sheer robe and carrying a box containing 12 video tapes. She took one out and walked over to the TV and took a tape out of the VCR and put it on top of the TV. She then slid the other tape in. When the picture came on it was Maria riding some dudes head.

"That's them," she said as she grabbed another tape. She slid it in and when it started it was Maria and a Mexican dude. Maria was standing up and the guy was eating her asshole out.

"That's my niece Sonia's baby's father. She's a good woman and she's just as beautiful as Maria. You'll see her at the funeral," she said.

Sin kept looking at the picture and realized it was Maria's cottage. When Janine took the other tapes back to her closet, Sin got up and put the tape on top of the VCR in.

"No wait!" Janine screamed as she came out. It was too late, and just as Sin thought, it was he and Maria. He started laughing. He had never seen himself on tape before and he liked it. He had to admit, he was fucking the shit out of Maria.

"You're not mad?" Janine asked as she stood in front of him.

"Nah, if that's what you like that's what you like," he said.

"You sure know how to make a girl feel it. I wonder how you would make a woman feel," she said as she let the robe fall to the floor.

"Look, Janine. I might be stupid for saying this while I'm in the room with a naked woman, but it ain't going down like that. I'm kinda sprung on Maria and I want to give her a chance. Don't get it twisted. I want to do some freaky shit to you, for real, but I ain't going to do Maria like that. Now she go bad on me, or we break up, I'll be on the first thing smoking!" he said.

"Baby, she will. She's not capable of having a monogamous relationship, and when she breaks your heart, and she will, don't say you didn't know. I'm not going to stop teasing," she said.

Sin started laughing again. "That works two ways," he said as he stood and walked to the door. He turned and looked at the naked goddess one more time. *"Damn!"* he said and walked out with a hard dick.

That girl better not fuck up with this one because he's a keeper, Janine said to herself as she turned and took the tape out and put a blank tape in and turned the TV to a station and flicked another button. The inside of Maria's cottage came into focus right at the point of the bed.

When Sin walked in he looked around where he thought the camera had to be for the angle of the shot. He barely saw it concealed in the vent in the ceiling over the bed. *You like to watch, huh?* He took his shorts and boxers off and started stroking his hard on. The phone rang.

"Hello!" he answered.

"You're not playing fair," Janine said.

"You weren't either. What're you doing?" he asked.

"The same thing you are," she said as his phone rang.

"Hold on," he said.

Sin grabbed his mobile and looked at the caller ID and saw Maria's number.

"Hello!" he answered.

"Baby, I'm at the gate. Push the red button on the phone." He did as asked.

"You ready for me?" she asked.

"For sho that," he said and hung up.

"I gotta go. Maria's here," he said to Janine and hung up.

He walked out to Maria's private gazebo and got in the hot tub.

When Maria came to the gazebo she found Sin kicked back.

"I hope you know I cut my night short because I was missing you," she said.

"I was missing you too," he said as he stood up and let her see how hard he was. Maria took her arms out of her dress and it fell to the floor leaving her naked. She then got in the hot tub.

"Sit on the edge," she said. Sin did as asked and Maria started sucking his dick. Maria was on the level with Shaunté and Yvette as far as giving head. She serviced him for like twenty minutes.

When Sin felt his nut coming he stopped her. He lifted her on the side and opened her legs and went down on her.

"Ooh yeah, Papi! Eat me my pussy!" she moaned. Sin made Maria cum and they got out of the hot tub.

"I wanna fuck, Papi!" she demanded. Sin lifted her up and she put her legs around his waist and he grabbed her ass cheeks and she guided him in. He pinned her against the wall and serviced her.

"You like that?" he asked.

"Yes, Papi. This is your pussy! Take it Papi!" she screamed. Sin carried her to the bed and put her knees to her shoulder and pounded the pussy. He turned her over and got her on her hands and knees and long dicked her.

"Damn, Baby! You got some good pussy!" Sin said as he pulled her hair.

"Harder, Papi!" she screamed. Sin slapped her on the ass and pulled her hair again. Maria's ass started vibrating and Sin held on as she started bucking. He couldn't hold his nut as he started going in as deep as he could. Sin wanted to pull out, but Maria was having none of that. He collapsed on her breathing hard.

"Ooh, Papi! Don't move! I'm cumming again!" Maria screamed. Once she finished trembling she lay there and listened to Sin's softer breathing.

"Baby," she whispered. She knew then she put him to sleep. She smiled and dislodged him. He opened his eyes and moved off of her back. Maria lay in his arms facing him and kissed his lips, which were only a half an inch from hers. *I'm falling hard for this nigga. I know he's really feeling me. I'm going to see how he acts and take this relationship one day at a time,* she thought as she fell into a peaceful sleep.

The ringing of the phone woke Maria. She looked over at the clock and saw it was 9:00.

"Hello!" she answered.

"You and your hot ass sister better get over here. Your appointments are for 10:00," the girl said.

"Krissy, we'll be there," she said to her cousin and hung up. Maria turned over and kissed Sin. He opened his eyes.

"Baby, I have an appointment at my cousin's shop at 10:00. It's going to take me forty-five minutes to get ready. So we got fifteen minutes to do whatever," she said. Sin didn't need to be told twice.

Chapter Thirteen

It Don't Stop

When they got to Oakland Tuesday, Maria dropped Sin off at his house. The first thing Sin did was call Shaunté to bring his truck. He then called June.

"Hello!" he answered.

"I just touched down. I need to talk to Malika," Sin said.

"She's with Simone and they were on their way to her mom's house after they stopped at Nation's downtown. Sin, don't go over that girls mama's house throwing a nutty," June said.

"A'ight," he said and hung up.

Sin heard the Navigator pull up and went outside.

"You got a little darker," Shaunté said as she walked up and kissed him.

"I missed your punk ass," he said as he hugged her.

"Baby, I been hella hot. Can I get some dick tonight?" she asked.

"We'll see. Has everything been going cool?"

"Hell yeah. I made over $300,000 for us."

"Give me 200 and you keep 100," he said.

"I knew you were going to say that. I got 200 in the

truck," she said. They walked over to the truck and got in and Sin pulled off.

"What the prices lookin' like?" he asked.

"The most I've heard is 20, but the average is 19," she answered.

"We going to dump them for 15-5 to June and Rod. Seventeen for everybody else. The ounces gon' go for 725," he said. They pulled up at the spot and Sin got out and hugged and kissed Shaunté.

"Baby, we need some more," she said.

"A'ight," he said as he got back in the truck. Sin had a funny feeling he was being watched. He looked around and didn't see anyone then he pulled off.

●●●●●●

"We can take this muthafucka in on the parole violation for not reporting, and we would be taking a lot of dope off the street," Perez said.

"Nah, I want him with the dope," Johnson said. "Tell unit two to be ready," he added as he pulled off. Perez picked up the Nextel.

"Unit two, he's coming your way," Perez said and hung up.

●●●●●●

When Sin pulled up at the light on 55th and MacArthur, a blue Grand Cherokee pulled up next to him. Inside was a cute, petite girl. She was dark brown skinned, had brown eyes, short styled black hair, and a cute face. She had some nice sized titties for a girl her size. She saw Sin checking her out and smiled. Sin rolled his window down.

"How you doing, sexy?" he asked.

"I'm alright, and you?" she asked.

"I'm a'ight now," he said as the light turned green and the car behind him blew it's horn.

"Ay, why don't you pull over at the 76 Station so I can talk to you," he said.

"Lead the way," she said. Sin pulled off and she followed. He made the left turn to the gas station and pulled in and she pulled in behind him. Sin threw the K-CI & JoJo CD in and turned the beat up and got out.

Damn, he cute! the girl thought.

The chick got out of the truck and Sin saw her body. She was 5'6" and about a 120 pounds. She was wearing a short, sexy blue dress. Her legs and thighs were big and sexy and she had a small waist, medium hips and a gang of ass. *God damn!* Sin thought.

"I'm Sin," he said.

"I'm Anita," she replied.

"Anita, you lookin good, baby. Can I get a number so I can schedule some time?"

"You looking good too, and my schedule has just became cleared. Let me see your phone," she said. Sin went to the truck and grabbed his phone. He handed it to Anita and she programmed her pager number in.

"So, when can I call?" he asked.

"Whenever you want to."

"A'ight, lovely," he said and got in the Navigator and cut to his mom's house to put the money up. He then left to the deep East.

Chapter Fourteen

Lost Love and New Findings

When Sin pulled up on 100th and Walnut at Malika's mom's house, he noticed the burgundy Tahoe with the Louisiana plates. He hadn't been over here since Malika's mom, Tina, tried to seduce him. He got out of the Nav and went to the door and rang the bell. Malika's Uncle Vince opened the door.

"What the fuck you want over here?" he asked. This might be the only other person Sin hated.

"Malika here?" he asked as he checked his temper.

"Man, you almost ruined that girl's life! Why can't you just stay the fuck away from her?" Vince yelled.

"Bitch ass muthafucka! Yell at your muthafuckin kids. Your punk ass yell at me again I'm going to serve you worse that I did when I was fifteen!" Sin yelled. Just then, Tina came to the door. She saw Sin and her eyes got big. Even though Tina hadn't spoken to him in the thirteen years Simone kept her up on what was going on with him.

Sin looked at Tina. At 43 Tina looked like she was still in her twenties. Her once long hair was cut short, her face was still beautiful, and her body was still banging.

"I ain't got time for this shit! She called me, I didn't call her," Sin said as he walked away. He got in his Nav and started it up just as Simone and Malika pulled up in Simone's honey gold SL500 convertible Benz on dubs. Sin looked in the passenger side mirror as Malika exited the car wearing skin-tight blue

DKNY jeans, a blue DKNY baby T-shirt, and some white DKNY tennis shoes. Malika still looked the same except she lost the baby fat. The last time Sin had seen her she was fine. Now she was beautiful. She stood at 5'10" and weighed 138 pounds. Her one quarter Philippine breeding gave her an exotic look. The rest of her was black. She was honey colored, had long black natural curly hair, slanted brown eyes, and big pillow like lips. She still had the same firm 36D's, 26 inch waist, and 38 inch hips and a big basketball ass. Sin started getting hard.

Simone got out next. Simone was a top notch too. She was a red bone with short Sandy brown hair, green eyes, and a cute face. She stood at 5'8", weighed like 145 pounds, and was thick as hell. She had 38DDD's, a tiny 24 inch waist, 38 inch hips.

As the girls were walking towards the house, Malika turned and looked over her shoulder. She saw Sin and grabbed Simone's arm.

"Is that… Sin?" she asked. Simone turned and looked.

"Yeah, that's him. Go get your man, girl," Simone said as she pushed Malika toward the truck.

Malika slowly came towards the truck. She titled her head and looked at him.

"You gon' just sit there?" she asked as she stopped in front of the truck.

Sin got out and walked to the front of the truck and hugged her. Malika held him tight as she started crying. Sin stepped back to look at her, and what caught his eye was her wedding ring. That messed him up. He stayed composed though.

"You didn't tell me you were married," he said.

"I'll be divorced shortly. Can we go somewhere and talk?" she asked as she wiped her eyes.

"Yeah, I know just the place," he said. They went towards the passenger side of the Navigator.

"Simone, I'll be by your house a little later," Malika told her.

Vince came walking off the porch towards the gate. "Malika, you bet not get yo' ass in there!" he yelled.

"Who the fuck you yelling at? I'm a grown ass woman and I'll do whatever the fuck I choose to!" she yelled. Sin opened the door for her and she got in.

Simone stopped him as he was going to the truck. "Baby Bro, I want you to promise me something, she said.

"Anything for you, baby," he said.

"Promise me you'll listen to everything she has to say and you won't nut up on her, and promise me you won't be mad at me, mama Jackie, or her. She's been going through some shit for a while, and she's really been having problems lately," Simone said.

"A'ight," he said and kissed her on the cheek. He got in the truck and pulled off. He put the Brian McKnight CD in and played *Anytime.*

"You would play this song now. I know you're mad at

me. So I'm going to let you say whatever you have to say first," she said.

He looked at Malika and shook his head. "Baby, I can't understand your reasons for not getting in touch with me. I ain't trying to hear that you tried shit. When you turned 18 you could've came back. I don't give a fuck who I was fucking with. I would've got rid of her for you. That makes me think for the one millionth time you didn't really love me, and if I had any sense I wouldn't be here talking to you. You fucked me up real bad," he said.

Malika's eyes filled with tears. "Sin, you need to go on with that bullshit. You know god damn well I loved you. You got another bitch pregnant while you were with me and I accepted it. I never asked you for no money or anything. I just wanted to be with you! Fuck! I was only 15, and I made the biggest mistake of my life when I gave up my fight to get back," she said as she noticed Sin pulled up at the San Leandro Marina.

"You remembered our spot," she said.

"I never forgot it."

"Me either," she said.

Sin noticed a black, unmarked police car pull up in the other side of the parking lot. He didn't pay it any mind, as he wasn't riding dirty.

"One of the reasons I came back is because I'm filing for divorce and I don't want to be in the same state as my soon to be ex. My job's relocating me out here. So I have two weeks to find a place to live," she said. Sin detected that there was something else.

"So, what was so important that you had to see me? You ain't been in touch with me in damn near fourteen years, why now, and what do what you said gotta do with me?" he sarcastically asked.

"Sin, you're about to be even more mad at me," she sighed. "I ain't gonna beat around the bush. It has everything to do with you. We have a thirteen year old daughter."

"What?" he said.

"Sin, please listen," she begged as she handed him the picture of his daughter. She looked just like him, but had Malika's body and tight eyes.

"I didn't know what to do. I wasn't about to get rid of my baby. I thought about giving her up for adoption, but when she came out she looked just like you, and I decided right there and then that I would do whatever I had to do to keep her and make sure she was safe," Malika pleaded.

"So you waited thirteen muthafuckin years to tell me I have a daughter? Are you out your got damn mind? What does she think, I left ya'll hanging or something?"

"No, she knows that we were forced apart. Sin, I was alone and confused. Then I came back out here on my 18th birthday and Simone told me you were fucking with some bitch. I don't know why, but that hurt my feelings. Mina knows about you. I have the picture we took at Corey's funeral reception. She made a copy and she keeps it with her. Sin, it was hard on me emotionally. My granny looked after Mina while I stripped at night to pay the bills, and went to school during the day. I did what I had to do for my baby," she said. Sin looked at her ring.

"So, when did you get married?" he asked.

"About four years ago. I didn't do it for love. I married Joe because I needed help. I've never loved him. I haven't been capable of love for a long time," she said.

Sin reached in the ashtray and grabbed the blunt.

"I'm getting a divorce for a few different reasons. First, because I got married for the wrong reason. Second, because he's abusive. He knows I don't love him. In fact I don't even like him. Third, because Mina's overdeveloped and I don't want to chance that something will happen to her. The girl has more body at thirteen than I did when I was *fifteen*!" Sin looked at the picture again. He knew he was going to have to hurt some young cat behind his daughter.

"And the fourth reason is because he wants a kid, and I'm not trying to be linked to him for life. I've had two abortions already. I can't have another one, and I refuse to have a child by him," she said.

"So you named her Mina?" he asked.

"No. What I tell you I was going to name the baby if it was a girl?" Sin smiled at Malika.

"You named her Simina," he said. Sin lit the weed. "So have you found a spot?" he asked as he passed the weed.

"I'm supposed to go check out a house in Dublin at three-thirty. I don't really want Mina going to Oakland schools," she said.

"You move way out there your ass going to be leaving at

six in the morning to get to work on time," he said.

"Shit, for this $160,000 a year I'll leave at *four* in the morning!" she said.

"It's damn near five now. I'll take you out there," he said as he started the Navigator and pulled off.

"So, Sin you gotta woman?" she asked.

"Yeah, I do," he said as he thought of Maria. "Oh Shit!" he said as he picked up his phone and speed dialed her.

"Hello!" she answered.

"When you come out here, I need 50 minutes of your time," he said.

"I'm picking up the keys to the house, and as we speak, Cynt and one of my cousins are supervising my stuff being loaded onto the truck. The only thing I'm arranging tonight is the bedroom and the family room," she said.

Sin looked at Malika. "I need to talk to you about something tonight," he said and hung up. Sin speed dialed Rod.

"Yeah!" he answered.

"Cuzzo, what you trying to do?"

"Twenty," Rod said.

"A'ight, I'm on my way to Dublin. I'll call you around nine," he said and hung up. He called June and found out he wanted fifteen.

When they pulled up to the house Sin was impressed. The house looked like every fourth house on the block. The landscaping looked nice and the street was clean. The house was an eggshell color, had a three car garage, and an area on the side of the house to store a boat. The back yard was huge, and it had a pool. The owner pulled up and they went in. The house was nice. There was an up and downstairs, a nice sized kitchen, dining room, and living room. An enormous family room, three bathrooms, and French doors led out to a patio. The three regular bedrooms were all the same size. The master bedroom was huge. There were double doors at the entrance, then you walk up four steps and you're in the living quarters. There were his and her closets to the right, and French doors to the left which led out to the terrace. There was a large space for bedroom furniture and there was a fireplace. You then walked down four other stairs and into the bathroom. There was a large Jacuzzi, his and her shower, his and her vanities, and a marble floor.

Sin walked up to Malika and the owner. "If she doesn't get it I'll take it!" he joked.

The owner wanted a $3,000 deposit, and $3,000 for two months rent in advance, but the house wouldn't be ready for two months because of a heating problem, and he didn't want to take Malika's out-of-state check.

"If I bring you a check for $9,500 and $9,000 cash tomorrow, can she move in sooner than that?" Sin asked.

"You bring me $18,500, she can move in tomorrow and just use the fireplace and I'll have the guy here to fix the heating within the week," he said.

Sin told the dude they would be back in the morning.

When they left Sin drove to the mall.

"Since you're a financial whiz, you think you can make some of my money right?" he asked.

"I know this lady that was one of my clients when I was a broker. She owned like 20 cookie stores all through the south. Well, I helped her to make a boat-load of money in stocks. About two weeks ago she called me and told me a major cookie company offered to buy her out. Sin, they offered her 65 million dollars for her recipes, the name of her company, and everything else involved. She told me she never had kids, and she looked at me as her daughter because of the way I looked out for her. Then she told me if I could come up with anything over $10,000 she would list me as someone that invested in her company and give me ten times what I put in back," she said. Sin started doing the math in his head. He had $200,000 he could invest, but that would be pushing him away from his goal of $3,000,000. He was almost at $1,000,000, as it was.

"Okay, this is what I want you to do. Find me a cool, black business lawyer or a Jewish one that don't ask a lot of questions. I'm going to give you 200 gees. One-hundred fifty-thousand for me, $50,000 for you. That should make me a mil and half and you a half mil," he said.

Malika stopped walking and just looked at him open-mouthed.

"You have $200,000?" she asked.

"Nah, baby. I gots *$800,000!* Come on now, *you* know how I move. You was with me when I stacked my first $50,000. The game ain't changed, the *players* did," he said.

"When do you plan to stop what you're doing?" she

asked.

"When I decide to," he said. They went in the furniture store and Sin bought Simina a bedroom set. He also bought them a wide screen TV for the family room, and 32" TV's for both their rooms. He bought everything they needed, except the dining room furniture, Malika's bedroom set, and the bathroom sets. Malika paid for all that. All the stuff was to be delivered the next day.

When they got to Sin's house they went in. He went straight to the back room to his stash spot. He pushed a chair over to the wall and took the vent screen off and reached in and grabbed a blue duffel bag. He took it to the table and unzipped it. He put thirty bound stacks of $10,000 on the table.

"Baby, look in that drawer and grab the plastic wrap," Sin asked. Malika had a flashback of when Sin used to give her a bag of money and be like, "count that". She brought the plastic wrap and he stacked the stacks on top of each other and she wrapped them up tightly. He then grabbed two more stacks, which equaled $20,000. He took $1,000 out of one of them and $500 out of the other and put it in his pocket. That left $18,500. He handed Malika $9,000, and put the other $9,500 in his inside coat pocket. He put the rest of his money back in the stash spot.

"I'll be right back. Don't answer the phone or the door," he said as he put the $300,000 in his coat under his arm.

●●●●●●

Sin walked out of the door, got in the Navigator, started it and pulled off.

He didn't notice the blue Ford Crown Victoria following

him. He smashed on the Warren Freeway and opened the Navigator up. He got off the freeway on Broadway Terrace, made a right, and drove up in the hills.

"Shit! We lost him! You think he saw us?" Johnson asked.

"Nah, Tony. If he saw us we would've known. We'll get back on him tomorrow," Perez said.

"Fuck it, I'm hungry! Let's go to Nations and get a burger. Then lets go rip up West Oakland," he said as he got off the freeway on Broadway Terrace and made a left and went back toward the flat lands.

●●●●●●

When Sin pulled up at Maria's there was a big moving truck out front, a Cinnamon colored 1999 convertible SL500 on 18" rims, the Black Expedition, and the silver Corvette in the driveway. He parked and got out and walked in the house while the ten Mexican dudes were moving the furniture in. Sin went to the bedroom where Maria was directing the guys where to put her stuff.

"Hey, baby!" she said and kissed him. She then turned to one of the guys. "Javier, go get the two boxes out of my truck and put them in my baby's truck," she said in Spanish.

"It's the green Navigator," Sin said in Spanish and handed him the keys.

"So, what do you want for dinner?" she asked.

"You know," he said and smiled.

"You can have that now," she said and kissed him again. He handed her the bag of money and she put it up.

"What time are you going to be home?" she asked.

"About 4:30," he joked.

Maria looked at him like he was stupid. "I wish you would try to play me like that! It would be on up in this bitch!" she said.

"I'll be here as soon as I go take care of some loose ends."

"If you see your brother, Terell, let him know he can't stay the night with Cynt. I'm not having that shit up in here," she said.

"A'ight," he said as Javier handed him his keys. Maria walked him to the door.

"That's your truck?" she asked.

"Yeah," he said.

"That's shit is *tight!*" she said. They kissed again and Sin left.

When Sin got to his house, Rod's blue '95 Honda Accord was there. He pulled into the garage and opened the back of the Nav and grabbed the boxes and counted the kilos. There were twenty-five in each box. All of them had the red scorpion stamp on the brown paper wrapping. Sin took 5 out of one of the boxes and put the 20 left in Rod's car in the front seat. He then grabbed an empty box and put 10 keys plus the odd 5 in for June. The 15 left were his. *For the 35 Rod and June are getting, I'll make $542,500. I owe Maria another $200,000. That leaves $342,000. Take $300,000 off that, since that's what I gave her. That means I made $42,500 plus 15 birds, which will make 297 gees,* Sin thought and smiled.

"I'm feeling myself for real!" he said out loud. He went in the house and Rod gave him the $310,000 then left. Sin put the cash up then he and Malika rode to June's and gave him the 15 and got the $232,500. They rode back to Sin's house.

"I'm making 297 gees just being the middle man," he said to Malika.

"Damn, you sure have stepped your game up!" she said.

"For sho, and once you help me legitimize and multiply this 200 gees, I'm going into real estate. Malika, I'm going to make it cool for all of us," he said.

Once the money was put up they left. Sin gave Malika the other $9,500.

"Give that to Simone and have her take you to see ol' boy and write a check for you for $9,500," he said as he pulled up to Simone's house. "I got some moves to make so I'll see you tomorrow," he said.

"Be careful!" she said as she got out. Sin smashed off. When he got to the light on 98th and Golf Links, he picked up his phone and scanned the phone book. When he came to Anita's number he pushed send.

"Hello!" she answered.
"Hey, beautiful! Do you know who this is?" he asked.

"No."

"This is Sin."

"Oh, hey. I didn't think you were going to call," she said.

"Can I see you tonight?" he asked.

"Yeah."

"Meet me at Mexicali Rose in like two hours."

"Okay."

"Bye!" he said and hung up. He speed dialed Tay.

"What's up, Boo?" she asked.

"What going down?" he asked.

"Rome called me trying get two and the spots are done. I picked up all the loot a little while ago," she said.

"A'ight, meet me at my house," he said and hung up.

When Sin got home he parked in the garage. As soon as he got inside he grabbed five keys and broke them down into 9 and 18 ounce packages. He grabbed two more and put them to the side for Rome. He then grabbed 100 gees and put it to the side. The 120 gees Shaunté would be dropping off would go with this 100 gees and would be the remainder of what he owed Maria.

He heard a car pull up. He went in the front room and

looked out the window and saw his SS Impala. He opened the door and Shaunté came in carrying four videotapes.

"I didn't tell you what the stupid ass bitch Juanda did. I sent her to the store to get a case of bags, and when she comes back she says she met a nigga, and she wants us to freak with him. I go smooth off on that bitch, and when I come out the kitchen to tell the guy he gots to raise up, I see Kendell from 84th. As soon as he sees me he gets spooked. He gets to stuttering and shit taking about, 'I d… d… don't want no problems with Sin, Shaunt… t… t... té!' I pull a fake nutty on Juanda telling her she done blew up my sister's spot so he don't know where I lay my head. Baby, he was hella scared. So I told him if he ever told somebody where my sister lived, I would tell you that he tried to rape me," she said.

"That bitch Juanda dumb as a box of rocks," he said as he pulled Shaunté close and kissed her.

"You wasn't trying to give up daddy's pussy?" he asked.

"No. And when you see how phony these bitches you fucking is, your ass will see the real me."

"You got my back?" he asked.

"More than you know," she whispered as she lay her head on his chest.

"Go get in the bed. I'll be there in a minute," he told her.

Shaunté pulled 120 gees out her coach and gave it to him, then hurried in the room. Sin put the $20,000 back in her purse.

When he entered the bedroom, she was lying in the

middle of the bed rubbing her pussy. Sin dropped his pants and crawled between her thighs and twisted her out for like 45 minutes. When they were done they both washed up.

Sin went and grabbed Maria's $200,000 and slipped one of the freaking tapes in his coat. When Shaunté came out they went outside and he put the 7 keys in the backseat of the SS. They then took the back streets to the turf. When they pulled up he kissed her.

"Go find us a little under apartment in Emeryville where we could keep the work. I don't like having that shit where we lay our heads," he said.

"A'ight. Am I going to see you tonight?" she asked.

"Nah, I'm getting money tonight. I'll see you tomorrow. It's something I need to talk to you about," he said as he carried the dope into the house. He kissed her again and left.

When Sin got to the Mexicali Rose, he saw Anita's Cherokee. He parked next to it and put his gun in the console and got out. The Mexicali Rose was the safest restaurant in the town. It was located across the street from the County jail, down the street from the police station, and within walking distance from the Fed building. A cat would have to be stupid to set some drama off there. Sin walked in and saw Anita at the bar.

"I hope you haven't been waiting long," he said as he sat next to her.

"No, I just got here about ten minutes ago," she said.

The hostess came and showed them to a table and a waitress took their drink orders.

"I'll have a Remy XO and the lady will have…"

"An apple martini," Anita said. She then looked at Sin. *Damn, he's fine!* she thought?

"So, what's up with you? You got a woman?" she asked.

"Nah, not really."

"What does that mean?"

"I'm not seeing anyone I wouldn't drop right now for you. What about you? You got a man?" he asked as their drinks came.

"No one serious," she said as she pulled out some money to pay for their drinks.

"Nah, I got it," he said as he pulled out a knot of money.

"No, baby. Kick back, I got this," she said as she handed the girl a $50 bill. *She get points for that,* he thought.

Sin sat back and drank his XO and stared at her.

"What?" she asked shyly.

"Girl, you look hella good," he said.

"Thank you. So what do you do?" she asked. Sin had his game down to a science when it came to dealing with legit chicks. He lowered his head in disappointment.

"I manage Michaels' Mobile Detailing, Window Cleaning

& Janitorial," he said sadly.

"Come on now. You ain't pushing no new Navigator detailing cars," she said.

"My brother owns it. I got money saved from back in the day when I use to do wrong," he said.

"So, you were a street star? I hear that's good cheddar. Why'd you quit?"

"I wouldn't say street star. I was doing a'ight though. I quit because I caught a case out of state, and before I was even sentenced, my girl had run off with the little money I had, got married and had a baby by another nigga," he said sadly.

"I know you wanted to kill her ass!" Anita said angrily.

Sin started laughing. "Nah I ain't like that. I just looked at it like all my dirt was catching up with me. It was my fault anyway," he said. Anita believed him. They sat and talked for the next hour then Sin walked Anita to her car.

"So, can I see you again?" he asked.

"I get off tomorrow at 6. Come by 24-Hour Nautilus tomorrow. I work out from 6:30 to 8:00."

"So what do you do?" Sin asked.

"I work for the City," she said as she got in her Cherokee.

Sin kissed her on the cheek. I'll see you tomorrow," he said as he went and got in his SS. She pulled out, and he went in one direction, and she went in the other.

When Sin got to Maria's, he parked across the street behind Terell's Iroc. He grabbed the bag of money and walked up the driveway. When he got to the door he rang the intercom.

"Who is it?" Maria asked.

"It's Sin, baby," he said.

"I'll be right there, honey." Within 30 seconds she opened the door. She stood there wearing a 2X blue striped, long sleeved shirt and panties. Sin kissed her and handed her the bag of money.

"You hungry, baby?" she asked.

"Yeah, for sure," he said.

"Go downstairs with Cynthia and Terell. I'll bring your plate down there," she said.

Sin went upstairs to the master bedroom, which occupied the whole top level. There were two bedrooms on the bottom level, along with a huge family room, two bathrooms, a fitness room, and a Jacuzzi. The main level had two more bedrooms, two bathrooms, a nice size kitchen, a formal dining room, a study/office, and a living room with a terrace. The top level was Maria's bedroom. She had a sitting room, two huge closets, a huge bathroom with his and her vanities, showers, and a three person Whirlpool. Every floor had a fireplace.

"Baby, your stuff's in the smaller closet," Maria hollered. Sin took his shoes off and hung his coat up. He then took his clothes off and put on some blue Girbaud shorts, then went downstairs.

"Don't forget to tell Terell what I said," Maria warned.

"Man, quit hating. I'm gon' to tell him," Sin said as he went downstairs.

When he came in the family room, Terell and Cynthia were watching TV and smoking.

"Man, if you trying to get somewhere, just bounce and wait down the street. I'll have Maria come to bed, then Cynthia can sneak out," he said.

"Big brother, you slick," Cynthia said.

"Girl, I ain't your brother. If your ass was older or I was younger I would take you down myself. That's for real" Sin said.

"Yeah right!" she said. *I would put this thing on your ass, and have you reaching for things that ain't even there,* she thought.

Maria came downstairs with a box of pizza. She sat it on the table then went and got two orange sodas out of the mini-fridge behind the bar. She sat down and they ate then smoked a blunt. Within twenty minutes Sin started yawning.

"Baby, I'm tired. Let's go to bed," he said.

"Bro, I'm gone. Cynthia, I'll be by here tomorrow morning to pick you up," Terell said as he kissed her. Sin walked Terell out.

"Bro, did you get some work?" Terell asked.
"Yeah, Tay got it. Man, while you going up in Cynthia,

hit that shit one time for me," he said.

"No doubt," he said and gave Sin a pound. He walked over to the Iroc, got in and left.

Sin walked into Maria's bedroom and got undressed. Maria got naked and threw on a light blue North Carolina jersey.

"You wanna watch a freak movie?" he asked.

"Yeah!" she said. Sin went and got the tape out his coat pocket and put it in the VCR.

"Oh, this some real shit!" she said as the screen showed Juanda lying on Tay's bed masturbating. What hit Sin was the date. He knew Shaunté and Juanda kicked it for the rest of the weekend after he left, but the date on the screen said June 14th. Sin's birthday was June 15th and they didn't kick it until after midnight, which made it the 16th. *I'll be damn! They were freaking before I got in the picture!* he thought. He knew then he would be marrying Shaunté.

On the screen, Juanda had just gotten off.

"You don't need to hold the camera. Come over here and suck my pussy," she said. The camera moved and was centered on the bed. Tay came into the picture, but her face wasn't visible, only her naked ass.

"Do you know them?" Maria asked as she watched Shaunté put on a strap-on.

"Just keep watching," he said. Shaunté walked over to the bed. Juanda started sucking the strap-on. Shaunté turned and looked at the camera.

Where have I seen that girl at? Maria asked herself? Then it hit her.

"Oh shit! That's your ex girlfriend!" she said. Shaunté pushed the remote and the camera zoomed in on Juanda's pussy and asshole from the back. She slid a finger in Juanda and Juanda started bucking back against her hand. The screen went back to normal and Shaunté threw Juanda's legs over her shoulders and fucked her like a man. After fifteen minutes they got in the 69 position and ate each other out for the next twenty minutes, then Juanda threw the strap-on on and served Tay doggie style.

The finale was Tay strapping on and fucking Juanda in the ass.

"Baby, I want to do that," Maria begged as she stroked Sin's dick.

"You serious?" she asked.

Maria didn't even answer. She let her head do the talking. Sin rolled over on top of her after ten minutes and he fucked her hard.

"So you gonna hook it up?" she asked.

"For sure. Can I join in?" he asked. Maria thought about it.

"As long as it's the Indian girl, and not your ex. Baby, you're my man and I want to satisfy you," she said. Sin kissed her and they went at it again.

When Sin woke up the next morning he jumped in the

shower. When he got out he lotioned his body up then put on blue boxers. He walked out onto the Terrace and saw that it was going to be a hot day. He went back in and put on his clothes he wore the day before. He brushed his teeth then checked his messages.

Sheree was still trying to talk to him. Bo called, Boss called, Yanna called, and J-Dub called. He called everything back that had to do with money. Boss wanted 20 keys, Yanna wanted one, and J-Dub wanted two. Sin went downstairs. Maria, Cynthia, and Terell were eating. Sin walked up to Maria and leaned down to her ear.

"I need to re-connect," he whispered.

"You have to go meet Javier. I don't want to start having that stuff in my house. I'll call him and tell him what you want, and you can just bring the money when you come home later," she said.

Sin sat down and ate. After he finished he got his gun and he left. He went home and put on some khaki Docker's, a white wife beater, a tan white and brown plaid short sleeved Sean John button up, and some walnut Tims. He slipped on the Movado, the 24"' solid gold link with the cross, the matching bracelet and diamond pinky ring. He put on his Channel clear lenses and the fitted tan Sean John cap, backwards. He called everybody and told them where to meet him.

As he was leaving Sheree pulled up.

"So when do you plan on talking to me?" she asked.

"I didn't plan on it," he said.

"So, that's how you carrying me?"

"You made it like this. So that's how you carried yourself," he said as his phone rang. He looked at the caller ID and at Tay's number.

"What's up?" he asked.

"Baby, I got a doctor's appointment. I'll call you and tell you when you can come get the rent money."

"A'ight," he said and hung up.

Sin looked at Sheree. "I got somewhere I need to be," he said as he opened his car door.

"What! You already messing with another bitch?" she asked angrily.

"Sheree, you said what you had to say on my birthday, so lets leave it at that. You ain't got my best interest at heart, you ain't got my back, and you ain't about to do what has to be done," he said.

"Yes, I am," she said.

"I'm going to Seattle tonight, and I need you to strap five birds on your body and get on the plane."

"Nigga, please! I ain't about to do no shit like that," she said. After she said it she knew it was a test, and she failed. Sin shook his head and got in the car. He started it and backed out of the driveway and left. He called Bo as he was in route to Choppy's.

"Hello!" he answered.

"I need to holla at you. Meet me at Choppy's on 48th and Telegraph," Sin said and hung up.

Chapter Fifteen

Time To Slow Down... For A Minute

When Sin got to the barbershop he saw his little homies, Jacob, Danté, and David, whom everyone called Davy, but Sin nicknamed him B.G. for Baby Gangster. Davy was from Seminary. Sin had known him his whole life. His auntie, Lottie, was the one who taught Sin the game. Davy's mom, Daphne, was a crack head and she didn't take care of Davy. Before Sin went to jail, he took Davy school shopping every year. Out of all the young Mad Circle kids, Sin favored Little Vic, who was Scatters protégé, and Davy. Lil' Vic was getting money tough while Scatter was in the Feds.

"Fuck you, you broke ass homeless muthafucka!" Jacob said to Davy.

"B.G., come holla at me," Sin said. Davy came over to the car. His clothes were wrinkled and he was in desperate need of a hair cut, but he was wearing some brand new Nike Air Max.

"Where your mama at?" Sin asked.

"I haven't seen her in two weeks," he said. Davy was 15 and stood at 6 feet even and weighed in at 180 pounds. He could actually pass for Sin's son. He was tall like Sin, same color, same eye color, and the same walk. The truth was, Sin was like a big brother to Davy and Davy tried to emulate his ways. Davy was looking grimy and Sin didn't like that.

"Nigga you want to come stay with me?" he asked.

"Yeah, if it's cool."

Terell and Cynthia pulled up in Maria's Expedition.

"Davy, you got that for me?" Terell asked him.

"Nigga, I know you ain't got him out here like that!" Sin asked angrily.

"I got all these niggas out here. And shit, he ain't got no where to go. He might as well be useful," Terell said. Sin wanted to hit him in the mouth bad. He looked at Davy.

"You got what you owe this nigga?" he asked. Davy nodded.

"How much is it?" Sin asked.

"Four-hundred," Davy answered.

"Keep it, B.G." Sin looked at Terell and shook his head. "Take it off that 5 gees you still owe me on that 5.0 I sold you."

"Bro, why you trippin?" Terell asked Sin.

"Nigga, when your moms booted you out, I gave you 5 zips (5 ounces), and paid your motel up for a month. You *front* him a half ounce and think you really doing something for him. From now on, I don't care what you do with these other lil' niggas, but this one with me. Come on, B.G.," Sin said. They walked in the shop and they got cut up.

When Yanna walked in the shop all eyes were on her body. Yanna wasn't the cutest girl, but she was thick to death. She was so light she was damn near white. She had medium length, thick light brown hair, dark brown eyes, thick eyebrows, full lips, braces on her teeth, and a scar under her eye. She was wearing a fuchsia colored dress that had her body looking "like that". She stood at 5'9" and weighed 130 pounds. She had firm 34C titties, a small 26 inch waist, 38 inch hips, a big sexy ass, and she was bowlegged. Sin could see by the way her dress was hugging her ass and titties she wasn't wearing panties or a bra. Sin and Yanna got down once the same month he went to jail while he was still with Yvette. Yanna was cold freak. She wore Sin out that night.

"What's up, sexy?' he asked.

Yanna sat the Macy's shopping bag down and walked over to Sin switching her ass and kissed his cheek.

"What's up with you?" she asked.

"Same ol' shit."

"When can a bitch get an encore?" she asked.

"You gotta get them eyebrows trimmed first. They was tickling my stomach last time," he said jokingly.

"Come on now, nigga. I wasn't complaining about when your side burns was tickling my inner thighs," she said joking back. The shop laughed at both of them. Sin paid Herb, the barber, and he and Yanna went and got in the SS. She discreetly slid Sin $18,000.

"I'm dropping the price to $17,000 tomorrow," he said.

"But for real though. When can I hit that again? I know you fuckin' with the crazy bitch, but I need some bomb ass dick in my life," she said.

"You down to take 10 keys on a plane for me?" he asked.

Yanna looked at Sin and contemplated the question. “You serious? Because the only person I’m with doing that for is my nigga. You trying to be my nigga?” she asked.

“No doubt,” he said.

“Then let’s go!” she said.

“I was just testing you, Boo. I’m happy being single. I do need another down ass woman in my corner though. I’ll be by your house tonight at nine,” he said as he slipped the kilo to her. She put it in her shopping bag then leaned over and kissed him.

“Until later then, daddy,” she said and got out the car. Sin put the money in the console. Davy came out and got in the car. Just then, Bo and his cousin, Marv, pulled up. Sin’s phone rang. He looked at the screen and saw June Bug’s number.

“What’s up, bro?” he asked.

“Lil’ bro, I need you to be at my house in 30 minutes,” he said.

“A’ight, I’ll call you back,” Sin said and hung up. He looked at Davy. “I’m about to make $165,000.”

‘Damn, bro! You be getting it,” he said. Bo opened the back door and got in.

“What’s up?” he asked as he gave Sin the $18,000 he owed him.

“How much dope you run through a week?” Sin asked.
“About 8 birds,” he said.

"If I shoot you 10 can you have my money by Tuesday?" Sin asked.

"Depends on the ticket," Bo said.

"Sixteen-5."

"Shit yeah!" he said.

"A'ight, I'll call you later on," Sin said.

"You ain't got nothing right now?" he asked.

"Nah," Sin said.

"A'ight, I'll see you later," he said. Bo got out the car and got in his burgundy, 1972 SS Nova with the white Rally stripes, and left. Sin sat there until J-Dub came. He gave him the two bricks and J-Dub gave him the $36,000.

Sin took his money home. He then took Davy to Bayfair Mall. He gave Davy $500, and while Davy shopped he called Maria.

"Yes, Papi?"

"I need 60 bucks."

"I got a 100 for you."

"I'm on my way."

"Meet me where you called me from the first day you came out here."

"A'ight" he said and hung up. After Davy finished shopping they left.

While in the car, Sin laid out the rules. "Look, nigga. You fixing to be going to school everyday, and summer school."

"Aww, maaan!" Davy groaned.

"B.G., the game ain't fixing to be here forever. If the game was over today a lot of niggas would be in trouble. I went to school everyday. First because I liked it. Second because that's where all the broads were at. I don't want you grinding dope, but I can't stop you from getting your money. I can make it easier though. I'll give $500 off every key you deliver for me."

"Cool! Now I can buy a car!"

"I'll get you a car. I don't want nobody to know what we doing. If you go to jail, keep your mouth shut. I'll handle it. Bro, don't ever go against the game," Sin said.

When they got to the house, Sin pulled up in the driveway. As he was getting out he noticed a green Ford Taurus pull up at the corner. They went into the house and Sin showed Davy to his room. Sin looked out the living room window and the car was still there and the two dudes inside were looking towards the house.

"Hell nah!" Sin yelled. He pulled his phone out and called Maria and told her he would hook up with Javier later. He then called Tay and remembered she had a doctor's appointment when he got no answer. He dialed the Seminary spot.

"Hello!" Lisa answered.

"Lisa, come by house. I want you to come the Maxwell Park way. It's a green Taurus parked at the corner. I think they the police. Don't stop here, meet me on the next block over behind my house," he said as he was looking out the window.

"Okay," she said and hung up. After Sin called Boss and June and told them he'd hook up with them after 7, he went in his stash spot and got his money and went in the garage and got the last of the dope. He put the 5 kilos in his backpack and put it by the back door.

Davy came out the bathroom wearing some white Girbaud shorts, a white red and green Nike Rugby shirt, some white and red Nike Air Max, and a white wave cap. Sin went in his room and got his Movado, his small link bracelet, and his Turkish rope with the diamond panther head. He took the stuff to the living room and gave it to Davy.

"That's 8 gees. You lose it, you buy it!" Sin said. He walked back to the window and saw Lisa's car turn the corner. His phone rang and he picked it up saw her number.

"What's up?" he asked.

"Sin, them muthafuckas are *definitely* the police!" she said.

"I'm on my way around there," he said and hung up. "Come on, we going out the back," he said to Davy. They grabbed the bags and Sin locked up. They hit the fence and walked down the path on the side of someone's house. When they came out, Lisa was pulling up in her olive green Acura TL. Sin slid in the back and Davy got in the front.

"Hit the freeway to Dublin," Sin said.

Lisa pulled off and rode straight to 580 going east.

"You lookin' good today, lil' daddy," she said to Davy.

"I'm living with my big bro now. I gotta represent," he said.

"When you turn 18, come see me," she flirted playfully.

"For what?" he asked. Sin tripped on Davy. He was game goofy when it came to broads. When Sin was 15, he was getting some cool change, and had more game than Milton Bradley. He would've never asked Lisa "what for".

"Bro, she saying when you turn 18 you can hit that," he said.

"Shit! Don't save mine. I want mine now!" he said.

Lisa started laughing hard. "First of all, I was only saying you look good, and when you grew up you'd be even finer. Secondly, I was just playing. Thirdly, I ain't going to jail for messing with you, honey," she said. Sin lit a blunt and passed it to Davy.

Sin's phone rang and it was a number he didn't recognize.

"What's up?" he asked.

"Sin, you coming out here today?" Malika asked.

"I'm on my way."

"My furniture's here, the phone's on, and the electricity

and cable will be on by 12:30," she said.

"That's cool," Sin said as he looked at his watch.

"I talked to your daughter today. I told her that her daddy got us a phat house and bought her all kinds of cool stuff. She wants to be on the next thing smoking up outta there," she said.

"Let her."

"I'm going to bring her back when I go out there to get my stuff. I ain't gonna lie, I'm scared as fuck. That muthafucka might try to kill me," she said.

"I ain't about to get in you and your dude's shit."

"Not even for your kid?" she asked.

Sin started laughing hard. "Man, I see your ass ain't changed. You hungry?" he asked.

"Yeah. Stop at the KFC and get me a chicken sandwich and strawberry soda," she said.

"A'ight" he said and hung up. "Stop at the KFC when we get off," he said to Lisa.

Sin was trying to figure out how the police got on his line. *One of these punk ass muthafuckas talking,* he thought. When they got off the freeway on Broder, Lisa pulled into KFC.

"Get me a chicken sandwich, an eighteen piece regular hot wings, some biscuits, and two large strawberry sodas," Sin instructed as he gave Davy $30. Davy got out and Sin got in the front. He knew he was going to be outta pocket for what he was about to do. He looked at the way Lisa's short pink and white dress had her big thighs looking.

"Lisa, when can I snatch you up and take you somewhere?" he asked.

"Sin, you know how Tay feels about you, and she's my best friend," Lisa said.

"Baby, we can keep this between us. She ain't gotta know," he responded.

"I've know Tay for 22 years, since pre-school, and that wouldn't be right," she countered.

Sin tried his luck. He touched her thigh and looked right in her eyes.

"Lisa, me and Tay ain't even together," he said as he saw that her nipples were poking through the dress.

"I know, but to her you're still her dude. If it wasn't her, I'd be on you," she said.

"What you got on under there?" he asked as he touched the bottom of her dress.

Okay, Sin you wanna keep playing? "A tiny g-string," she said.

"So, I can't fuck?" he asked as he rubbed her thighs. Lisa surprised herself when her legs slightly parted as if they had a mind of their own.

"It ain't going down," she whispered.

"Well, can I at least see how many licks it takes?" he asked. When she hesitated, Sin knew he had her thinking. "Baby, I know your ass is a head freak. I also know Tay showed you the tape me and her made when we were in Monterey. You know how I do it," he said.

Lisa's thong got wet just thinking about how Sin worked Shaunté with his fingers, tongue, and dick.

"Sin, you putting me in a uncomfortable position, and you making it hard for me to say no, but you're my girls sunshine, so that makes you off limits," she sighed.

"I keep telling you I'm not with her," he said.

"But you know how she feels. Shit, in her eyes you and God almost neck and neck," she said.

"What about your eyes?" he asked.

"I can't lie, I used to have a crush on you when ya'll first got together."

"So you don't want to test out this tongue?" he asked. Sin saw Lisa was losing to temptation. He leaned over and kissed her knee, then licked between her thighs all the way up to her panties.

"Sin, why you doing this to me?" Lisa whined.

"Because I want you, baby," he said. Just as he was sitting up, Davy was coming out KFC. He slid in the back and they left.

Sin gave Lisa directions to Malika's. When they got to the house, Davy got out and Sin looked at Lisa and licked his lips.

"I'm not going to stop asking," he said.

"You wrong, Sin," she said.

He got out and he and Davy went to the door. Malika opened the door wearing some tight blue Baby Phat shorts, a white Nike sports bra, a blue short sleeved shirt which was unbuttoned, and some white Nike flip flops. Her curly hair was blown out straight, and went down her back. When Davy saw her he stood bug-eyed with his mouth open.

"What's up?" she asked and walked away ass bouncing.

"*Damn!*" they both said.

"I see some things ain't changed," he said.

"Oh, they changed. You just ain't seen them, yet," she said as she put a extra shake in her hips.

"Bro, I gots to get the kind of loot you got. Every woman you mess with is top notch," Davy said as they walked in.

"B.G., that one there and Shaunté were with me when I was broke. That's my baby mama. She used to keep you when you was a baby," Sin said as they walked upstairs to Simina's room and he put the 5 keys of powder in the closet.

"Malika, this is B.G.," Sin said.

"What does that stand for?" she asked.

"Baby Gangsta," Davy said.
"I should've known," Malika said.

"You might remember him by 'Little David'," Sin said. Malika looked at Davy again.

"Oh my god! Boy, the last time I saw you, you were just learning to walk. You was with me so much people thought you were my baby. Well, anyway I'm glad ya'll here. Ya'll can move this furniture around for me," she said. Sin and Davy looked at each other and sighed and got to work.

While Malika had them moving her stuff where she wanted it, the doorbell rang. She went to the door. Then, Sin's phone rang.

"Hello!"

"Sin, I need you to pick your son up from school at 12:00," Tracy said.

"I'll pick him up, but he can't stay the night. I think the police are watching me," he said.

Tracy sighed. "Man, you act like you like being in jail or something, Sin," she said angrily.

"What the fuck you mean? Don't be coming at me with that stupid shit. What the fuck wrong with you?" he yelled.

"Sin, you better quit fuckin yelling at me! Every time your stupid ass goes to jail, I'm the one there for you, taking care of everything, and I'm fuckin tried of it! Because of you, I'm incapable of having a healthy relationship with another man!" Tracy cried.

Sin calmed down a little. Tracy hardly ever cried, and

when she did it was because something was bothering her. Sin made Tracy the woman she was. She was the true definition of a down ass bitch. The only thing Shaunté had on her was Shaunté would get down and do dirt with her man. It was nothing to her to park the Lexus and take off the Versace dress and throw on some jeans and a hoodie and get on the block, or to go kill a muthafucka. She was cut like that.

Yet and still, Tracy held him down while he did his bid in the ATL, and he would be forever in her debt.

"You mad at me because I want to make sure my babies and their mamas are okay? Tracy, there are three things in this world I know how to do real good. They are making money, taking care of my family, and fuckin. You living with a nigga and I'm still breaking bread with you. You benefiting like a muthafucka," he said.

"Sin, it ain't even about the money. I done been down with you when you were at your lowest," she said. Just then Malika came back in.

"Look, I'm busy. I need to talk to you about something later. Make sure you're around."

"You just make sure you pick my son up," she said.

"I'll pick my son up," he said and hung up.

Malika looked at him. "Girl problems?"

"Nah, baby mama drama!"

"I heard you say *he* couldn't spend the night. That was a mistake, right?" she asked.

"I thought you knew. I have a seven year old son and another 4 year old daughter," he said as he pulled his wallet out and gave it to her. She opened it. There was a picture of Tracy with Malik and Quesha, a picture of Tracy and Malik when he was a baby, a picture of Malik by himself, one of Quesha by herself, one of Kesha and Quesha when she was a baby, one of him and Shaunté, one of Simara, and one of Shaunté by herself.

"He looks just like Mina. Who's she?" Malika asked.

"That's Shaunté. She pregnant by me," he said. Malika threw the wallet on the bed.

"Nigga, you fuckin everything walking," she said angrily.

Sin looked her up and down. "Nah, Boo, not everything," he said.

"Nigga, please. I had the dick before, *anybody*. I was the *first*. I made that muthafucka what it is now," she said with an attitude. Davy snickered.

"Man, you can miss me with the hoe ass attitude. If your punk ass would've been a real woman, they would all be by you," Sin said angrily.

"I wasn't a woman! I was a scared 15 year old girl, by myself! If your punk ass was a man you would've found me!" she said even more angrily.

"So you tryin to say all this shit is *my* fault? You stupid than a muthafucka. If your dumb ass called mom's house, or Lottie's everything would've been cool," he said.

"Nigga, if your mama *told* you I was calling, you

wouldn't have said no dumb ass shit like that!" she said. Sin was about to say something but changed his mind.

"Can I get a ride to Oakland? I gotta pick my son up at 12"

Malika looked at her watch and saw it was 11. After the cable man left they went and hit the freeway. When they got to Oakland they still had 20 minutes to kill. Malika went by the key shop and had 3 sets of keys made to the house. She gave Sin a set, one set would be for Simina, and one for Simone. They went and picked Malik up, and Malika fell in love with him. They dropped Davy off on 49th then went to Sin's mama's house.

"What you doing later?" Malika asked.

"I don't know. Why?" he said.

"Because, I ain't tryin to be up in that big ass empty house by myself," she said.

"I can't stay the night. I got a woman," he said.

"So what that mean? I ain't asked you to let me hit that. I said I didn't want to stay by myself."

"I'll come check on you, but I ain't staying," he said as he and Malik got out the car.

Malika pulled off looking at Sin through the rearview mirror. "I'll have that ass back, and I'm sure of that" she said out loud.

Sin and Malik went in the house.
"What's up, Princess?" he said to Quesha.

"Nothing," she said as she kissed him.

"Daddy, I want to go see my mama," Quesha said.

"A'ight, lil' mama, hold up. I'll take you," he said.

"Thank you, daddy." He went to the kitchen where his mom was.

"Why did you send Malika's letters back, and didn't tell me she was calling here?"

Jackie knew the day would come for her to have this conversation with Sin.

"Simian, you were only 15. You were too young to be a father, and that girl's mother was talking about having you arrested for statutory rape if you tried to go get her daughter, and attempted murder for shooting her house up while her and her other kids were in it. You were my child and I did what I had to do to protect you," she said.

"Did you ever think of what I would look like to my kid?" he asked.

"I wasn't thinking about anything but *my* kid--you!" she said.

"I wasn't even living here. You kicked me out, remember? Mama, you was wrong. I missed all 13 years of my daughter's life," he said disappointedly.

"Well, what you and Malika don't know is on every one of that child's birthdays, I gave Malika's mother a cashier's check for $2,500," she said.

Sin turned and walked out the kitchen and went to his sister, Kim's old room. He removed the paneling in the closet and opened the safe and got the $100,000 he had in there.

"If Tracy gets here before we bet back, tell her to put this in her trunk," he said and he put the five bags of money behind the couch.

Chapter Sixteen

They Shoo... Shoo... Shooting!

Sin and the kids got in the dusty K5 and went to Burley's Detail Shop and got the truck done. When they left, the truck was sparkling. They hit freeway and went to the East.

Sin parked on Havenscourt and Bancroft and got out. He saw a cute girl and walked up to her.

"Ay, Boo! You know Kesha?" he asked.

"Yeah. Who is you?" she asked.

"Her baby's daddy."

"Man, I suggest you go rescue her from that nigga she messing with."

"Why?" Sin asked.

"He got major work and he letting her sit up in there and get high all day."

"I feel you, but where she at?" he asked.

"Down the street on 68th right off Arthur. Follow me and I'll show you," she said. She got in a raggedy 86 Honda. Sin got back in the K5 and pulled off following the chick.

When they got to Arthur a block away, the girl signaled Sin to pull over. He got out and walked up to her car.

"It's around the corner. The pink house on the left with a

black Maxima in front. You got something?" she asked. Sin looked at the chick disappointedly.

"You fuck with dope?" he asked.

"Sometimes," she said embarrassed.

"Come on, baby girl. You way too pretty for that shit," Sin said as he looked in her eyes. He saw the early signs of her drug abuse, but she was indeed still fine. It wasn't too late for her, but it would soon be.

"What's your name?" he asked.

"Jamila," she said.

"Well look, Jamila. I ain't got no yay, and when you ready to get right holla at me. My name's Sin. That spot on Bromly is mine. I got a job for you making some *real* loot," Sin said as he handed her a $50 bill and his number. He got into the K5 and pulled off.

Jamila knew some shit was about to jump off so she went and parked on the corner.

When Sin pulled up in front of the house he just shook his head. There were abandoned cars parked across the dried out grass, beer bottles all over the place, trash on the ground, and boarded up windows. He got out and went to the door and noticed it was barely on hinges. He knocked on the door.

"Who is it?" a female asked.

"Hey, is Kesha here?"
"Who wants her?"

"Tell her that her baby's daddy out here," Sin said.

"Tell him she ain't here," a male voice ordered.

"Man, I ain't fixing to be out here playing no hoe games with you muthafuckas! I'll tear this bitch up!" Sin said.

"What that punk ass nigga say?" the dude asked loud.

Sin stepped back and booted the door off the hinges and went in. A light skinned nigga pulled out a 9mm and pointed it at him. He was like 5'8" and weighed 180. He had a short faded hairstyle, green eyes, and a mouth full of gold fronts.

"Nigga, do you know who the fuck I am? I'm Max. J.B. my brother," he said. Sin had heard of Max. He had a few spots crackin' and was reputed to be a straight fool. His money wasn't as long as Sin's though. His brother, J.B., was a whole other story. He was having money like June and Rod. Sin remembered that June and J.B. were at war a few years back.

"Nigga, that gun shit don't faze me," Sin said. Just then Kesha came out looking halfway like the old her. Her hair was whipped, her nails done, and she was fitted. Sin saw the pipe in her hands. When she saw Sin she got scared.

"Max, what you doing?" she asked. She looked at Sin again. "Just go, please!" she said.

"Go see your daughter. She out in the car," he said, still looking at Max.

"I'll come by Miss Jackie's and see her later," she pleaded.

"Man, you know what? You ain't gotta never come see her!" he said as he turned to leave.

"Hold up, muthafucka! You fixing to pay for that door. Empty your pockets and break bread!" Max said. Kesha looked in Sin's eyes and knew he was going to kill Max.

"Max just let him go. You about to start a…"

"Kesha, take your ass in the room," he yelled. Kesha was about to say something else. She shook her head and went back to the room. Sin took the $700 he had in his pocket out and threw it on the floor.

"Nigga, take the jewels off too!" Max yelled. Sin took off all his jewelry and threw it on the floor. He looked at Max and went out the door. As he was going to the truck he saw Jamila.

"Get from around here," he said as he got in and pulled off. He picked up his phone and made a call.

●●●●●●

"Max, what the fuck is wrong with you? You just robbed Sin! He's going to come back shootin'!" Kesha yelled.

Sin? Where do I know that name from? Sin? He dropped the Rolex and the smile left his face.

"Please say you ain't talking about Sin from the Mad Circle," he said.

"Who the fuck else named Sin you done heard of?" she yelled.

"Kesha, you gotta take this shit back and let dude know I didn't know!" he pleaded.

Kesha, picked the money and jewelry up and went to the garage and got in Max's blue '97 Suburban and pulled out and left. Max picked up his phone and dialed.

"Yeah!" the voice answered.

"J.B., I just got into it with that nigga June bug's brother, Sin," he said.

"Man, fuck them hoe ass Mad Circle niggas. Where you at?" J.B. asked.

●●●●●●

Sin saw Kesha when she pulled off in the Suburban.

"Daddy, there goes my mama," Quesha said.

"She's gong to come to your granny's and see you tomorrow," he said. Sin was so mad he couldn't concentrate. Terell and Cynthia pulled up behind the K5, followed by a tan four door '78 LTD.

"Ya'll come on. Cynthia's going to take you back to granny's," he said as he got out. Sin walked the kids over to Cynthia's black '98 convertible Camaro Z-28. He put the kids in and she drove off.

"I bought your MP5," Terell said as he nodded to his boy, Mike, to open the trunk. Mike opened the trunk and Sin grabbed the MP5 and two clips. He pulled his phone out and called Tracy and told her to report the K5 stolen.

"Let's go," Sin said. Terell picked up his Mac 11 and they drove down the street. Sin pulled up on the grass and jumped out. Mike and his boys pulled up in the middle of the street and got out too. Someone had nailed the door back up. Terell kicked it in and they rushed in. A dope fiend chick stepped out.

"What the fuck ya'll think ya'll doi…" She never finished her sentence because Sin hit her in the chin dropping her like a sack of potatoes. Sin heard movement in the kitchen and ran in there. Max let three rounds off at him. Sin ducked back behind the door. He stuck the MP5 in the doorway and let six rounds off nearly hitting Max. Mike ran through the door shooting his AK in a sweeping motion. Max ran straight through the wooden screen door. Sin saw him running on the side of the house. He started shooting through the walls as he ran through the house. When he and Terell got to the front door, Max let off eight shots from behind one of the abandoned cars. Sin and Terell ducked back in. Terell nodded and he and Sin walked out spraying. When their guns ran empty Max stood up and let off his last two wild shots then ran. As he was hitting the corner Mike started shooting at him.

"Fuck!" Sin yelled as he watched Max get away.

"Come on! We up outta here," he said as he ran to the truck and he and Terell left.

Sin rode to the Seminary spot and pulled in the back yard. He and Terell got all Sin's music and personal stuff out of the K5. Lisa and Déja came out.

"What's up?" Lisa asked.
"I just had a shoot out with that nigga Max from 56th

Street. Ya'll be careful," he said. "Lisa, don't you know how to steal cars?"

"Yeah, why?" she asked.

"Hot wire this," Sin said. Lisa went to the K5 and looked in Sin's tool box and grabbed a hammer and a screwdriver. She popped the ignition off and stuck the screwdriver in the steering column and started the truck. Sin wiped down the inside. They rode to the store on Seminary and Foothill and left the truck there.

Sin's phone rang as they were walking back to the spot. "Yeah!" he answered.

"Sin, this is Kesha. Where you at?" she asked.

"Tell that bitch ass nigga I missed this time, but his life ain't worth the jewelry he got me for," he said.

"What did you do? I'm at your mom's with your stuff!" she yelled.

"Stay there," he said and hung up.

"Call Cynthia and have her pick us up at the spot," he said to Terell. Sin called June and told him what happened. "Come by mama's. I'll be there in forty-five minutes," Sin said and hung up. Sin looked at his watch and it was 2:30.

When they got back to the spot, the little chick, Jamila, was there.

"I thought about what you said," she said.

"So what? You ready to get some money?" he asked.

After they were done talking, Sin gave her his mobile phone number.

When Cynthia came, Sin had her drop him off at his mom's. When they pulled up, Tracy was there. Kesha was standing in front of the Suburban talking to Quesha. Sin took Malik in the house then came back out and saw Kesha hugging Quesha.

"Princess, go in the house. I need to talk to your mama," he said.

"Okay, Daddy," she said and went in the house. Sin walked up to Kesha.

"I'm gon' tell you some real shit. I'm gon' have your boy's head. I put that on my kids. Dude is a wrap," Sin said.

"Why is you trippin? I got this shit back for you," Kesha said calmly as she handed Sin his money and jewels. "I know what it is. You don't want to see me happy for shit!" she said angrily.

"Bitch, just a couple of months ago you were about to get your head split over $15. When I came up in that raggedy ass spot you had a base pipe in your hand and you didn't want to see your daughter. How the fuck's that happy?" he yelled.

"Your punk ass always talking about me smoking dope. What about you? Your ass selling it! You ain't no better than me," she said just as June pulled up in his coke white 600 coupe.

"You trifling ass bitch! I'm keeping a lot of muthafuckas fed. Nobody in my bloodline, Circle, or affiliated with me is going hungry. Bitch, I taught your ass the game and you took it and ran backwards. Our daughter stays clean and laced in nothing but the best. And speaking of which, when was the last time you spent some time with her, or better yet just came to see her?" he asked.

Kesha tried to throw a nutty, but Sin wasn't impressed. He had seen it all and heard it all when it came to her.

"Nigga, I would see her everyday if you and that bitch didn't get the courts involved," she yelled. Sin noticed the neighbors standing outside. Sin was about to go hard but Tracy came busting out the house.

"I got this, Sin. Bitch, that was all Sin's doing, and I'm glad he did it, before the Child Protective Services had taken her," Tracy said.

"Fuck you, bitch! You stole my family!" Kesha yelled.

Tracy sucked her teeth. "Hoe, get that shit right. Sin chose *me!* I wouldn't even fuck with him at first because he was with you. What made me start messing with him was me seeing you one night on East 14th with hella crack heads at 3:30 in the morning. I'm a real woman. I didn't hate and tell on you. I went on and hooked up with him. Then as far as Marquesha goes, *you* ain't been a mother to her. You put *dope* before her. As far as I'm concerned, *I'm* Quesha's mom. Shit, I'm the one that has taken care of her since she was 4. Where the fuck was you during the chicken pox, rashes, fights, flu's, homework, and field trips?" Tracy yelled.

"Bitch, who the fuck you think you talking to? You think the sun rises and sets on this niggas ass. You were just a rebound bitch! Why you think he dumped you after he put that little bastard in you?" Kesha yelled.

Sin slapped Kesha so fast she didn't see it coming.

"Hoe, don't you ever talk bad on my son again!" he said.

"Granny!" Quesha screamed from the door. June grabbed Sin and held him back. Tracy rushed Kesha and they fought. Kesha had hands, but Tracy had them too. Quesha ran out the house and tried to get between them. Sin pulled her back.

"Mama!" she screamed. They stopped and Quesha broke away from Sin and ran straight to Tracy. That fucked Kesha up.

"Baby, I'm going to come get you Friday," Kesha said.

"Daddy, I don't want to go!" Quesha cried.

"Oh, you ain't going. Kesha, get up outta here," he said.

She walked over to the Suburban and got in and looked at her daughter and left. Tracy took Quesha into the house. Sin told June what all happened. June got in his Benz and left.

Tracy came back out with the bags of money.

"Take me to Seminary," he said as he took the money and put it in her trunk. They got in the new, brown Acura and left.

"You remember when I told you about that chick I was in love with then I was 14?" he asked.

"Yeah, what about her?"

"She's back, and just told me she had that baby," he said.
"Sin, don't go out sideways. She probably heard from

Simone you were on top, and now she's trying to get a piece of the pie," Tracy said angrily.

"She's a junior partner at J.A. Drake. She don't need my money. Then I couldn't deny this one if I wanted to," he said as he showed Tracy the picture.

"Oh shit! Baby, she looks just like Malik," Tracy said.

"I gotta lot of making up to do," Sin said as his phone rang.

"Hello!" he answered.

"Baby, I'm sitting here naked playing with myself," Maria said.

"I'll be there in a second," he said and hung up.

While en route to Seminary, Tracy told Sin she was moving. Sin leaned over and put one arm around her neck and one in between her thighs.

"So you going to let me come break the new spot in?" he asked.

She started laughing. "Boy, move before you make me tear my car up."

"For real though, Poodah," he said.

"You haven't called me that in hella long. But for real, I ain't fucking with you. Your ass ain't gon' have me waiting for you and you don't show up like you did in Reno."

"I just wanna be the first to break in the furniture I'm

buying you," he said as they pulled in front of the spot. Sin went and got his music and stuff out the spot and put it in Tracy's trunk. He took fifty 10 gee stacks of his money and put it to the side. He took another 10 gee stack and gave it to Tracy. "That's like 500 gees in the trunk," he said.

"I'll be careful," Tracy said.

"Take me to get a rental," he said. Tracy took Sin to Executive Rental, where he rented a silver ES400 Lexus. He then kissed her and went on his way.

Chapter Seventeen

Outsmarting the Po' Po'

When Shaunté pulled out of the Piedmont Lane Apartments parking area where she was checking on a spot, she saw a black, two door Explorer pull out behind her. *Did I see them pull up when I got here? Maybe I'm trippin,* she thought. She stopped at the light on Piedmont and MacArthur. When the light changed she made a left. She saw that the truck made a left too. She went over the overpass merging to the freeway. The Explorer did the same. *If these muthafuckas take the same exit I take, I know they following me,* she thought. She took the Edwards exit and rode it until it turned into 73rd. As soon as she saw the Explorer come over the hill, she speed dialed Lisa.

"What up, bitch?" Lisa asked.

"Meet me on the movie side of Eastmont Mall. Somebody's following me," Shaunté said.

"I'm on my way," she said and hung up. "Déja, take me to get Tay. Somebody's following *her* now," Lisa said as she grabbed her Coach bag. They ran outside and got in Déja's Camaro and went to get Tay.

When Shaunté pulled up at the front entrance to the mall, the Explorer parked not too far from her. Shaunté looked out the corner of her eye as she walked to the entrance. She saw that one of them was white, the other was Mexican. *Shit! They the goddamn police!* she thought. She looked around for a little while and after ten minutes her phone rang.

"Bitch, where you at?" Shaunté asked.

"We just pulled up. Come on," Lisa said. Shaunté hung up and looked around then paid to get in the theater. She went in and some bootleg movie was playing. She sat in the top row and waited. No one came in. She got up and walked down to the emergency exit, and out the door. Once her eyes adjusted to the light she saw Déja's Camaro. Shaunté walked over and Lisa opened the door and she slid in the back.

"Go around to the front. Them muthafuckas the police!" she said as she sank down in her seat.

"I had to go pick Sin and B.G. up earlier. The police was following him too. They followed him to his house," Lisa said.

"Shit!" Shaunté yelled. She pulled her phone out and dialed Sin's mobile as they passed by the Explorer.

"Yeah, that's the po' po'," Lisa said as she saw Local (E) on the plate which meant it was a law enforcement vehicle.

"Go to my house. I gotta get everything outta there," she said to Déja.

"What's up, lil' mama? Sin answered.

"Baby, the police following me. I just shook they assess in the mall. I'm on my way home to get that money and them heaters up outta there," she said.

"Fuck! Tay, pack you a bag and put that suit on. You going to Reno to your sister's until the 4th of July," he said.

"So where you want me to meet you at?" she asked.

"I'll be through there. Have Lisa take your loot and the

heaters to her house. Then have her have somebody go get your car."

"Okay" she said.

●●●●●●

Sin pulled up at Yanna's dope spot. He called her on the phone.

"What's up, Boo?" she asked.

"Come downstairs," he said and hung up. *One of these rat ass muthafuckas is gon' get they shit knocked off they shoulders,* he thought as he saw Yanna coming down the stairs in some tight, pink low rise Baby Phat velour sweats and a white wife beater.

"I'm breaking her back tonight," he said. Yanna opened the door and got in.

"Baby, I'm going to need you to step up to the plate tonight. What time you going home?" he asked.

"When you tell me too, baby," she said.

"I'll call you as soon as I go pick up some work," Sin said.

"You staying the night with me?" she asked.

"Not tonight, baby. I am going to come back and hit and lick something though," he said as he suggestively licked his lips.

"Nah, daddy. Save that licking shit for when you gon'

stay all night. I want some of that bomb ass dick!" she said.

Sin pulled his phone out and called Maria.

"Hey, Papi!" she said.

"Call your boy and tell him I'm in Tracy's and I should be there in 30 minutes," he told her.

"Sin, what about me?" she whined.

"Maria, I'm trying to get this money right," he said.

"Sin, you better be here by 7!" she said and hung up.

"I'll be back in 30 minutes. Be ready you going with me to Modesto," he told Yanna. She leaned over and kissed him and got out. Sin pulled off fast.

As Sin was getting on the freeway, he was in deep thought. He knew without a doubt somebody was telling. He decided then that he was going to start cutting people off. If they weren't in The Circle, they were suspect. Then they were following Tay too and that really messed with his head.

As he was pulling up at Shaunté's, he called her to let her know he was pulling up. The gate swung open and he pulled in. He looked round and didn't see anyone, but knew that didn't mean anything. He got out the car and hurried into Tay's apartment. When he came in, Shaunté was sitting in the living room. Sin didn't know what it was about her, but he knew he was gone on her.

"Baby, somebody's running their mouth," she said.

Sin sat down next to her. "I know, but I can't think of who. Me and you ain't serving nobody. My clientele can fuck with Lisa, Terell, or B.G.," he said as he lay his head in her lap and kissed her stomach.

"B.G.? I know you ain't got B.G. on the block!" she said as she angrily pushed his head away.

"That nigga gon' hustle whether he get the shit from me or somebody else. But no, I ain't got him grinding. I'm giving him 500 for every bird he drop off for me," he said.

"I guess that's okay. Daddy, how long I gotta stay in Reno?" she asked.

"Just get out the way for a week or two," he said.

"Can I hit something before I go?" she asked and rubbed his dick. Sin wanted to fuck her bad, but he had business to handle.

"I'll come out there tomorrow," he said and kissed her. She went and got the bag of money and handed it to him.

"That's 125 gees," she said.

"The $25,000 is yours," he said.

"Keep it for me," she said as she straddled him.

"Unh Unh, boo. We gotta get," he said. They got up and he grabbed her two suitcases and the bag of money then left.

"Call me when you get there," he said as he loaded her stuff into her Yukon.

"Okay," she said as she kissed him and pulled off. Sin went to Tracy's and left the 100 gees. He then got on the freeway and went to Yanna's. He had her follow him to Modesto.

After they connected with Javier, and were on 580 in Dublin coming back, he called Boss and told him to meet him on Yanna's block. When they counted Boss' money there was 310 gees. Sin put that with the 500 gees he had and it totaled $810,000. He jumped on the freeway and went straight to Maria's house. When he pulled up in her driveway it was 7:30. He found the front door open and walked in. He went to Maria's bedroom and she was standing in front of the mirror fully dressed.

"You were suppose be here a half hour ago," she said.

"I had to handle my business," he said.

"What, your business is more important than what I gotta do?" she asked angrily.

"So, I can't get no pussy?" he asked.

"Nigga, if your ass wanted some *pussy,* you would've gotten here when I told you to," she said.

"Man, take that shit off!" he said playfully. Maria looked at him like he was stupid. She thought about saying something slick just to get a rise outta him.

"Sin, get out," she said as she glared at him.

Sin was getting irritated. "Man, I ain't about to kiss yo' ass for no pussy. Bitches selling they souls for some of this dick," Sin said as he tossed the bag of money at her feet.

"You calling me a bitch?" she asked as she took her earrings and heels off like she wanted to fight.

"I only call it like I see it, and right now you acting like a bitch up in this muthafucka," he said angrily.

"Nigga, fuck you! We ain't even got to be together!" she said.

"We damn sure don't. Just make sure you honor our deal," he said.

"And if I don't?" she boldly asked.

Now Sin was mad. "If you done had me get that money off Don, *and* had me handle them Colombians and think you gonna fuck off our deal, I swear, I'll make you wish you was dead," he said seriously. The way Sin was talking to Maria turned her on. *We'll just see how far I can go before he snaps*, she thought.

"Them threats ain't scaring me. You ain't the only one who will bust their gun. I'll have your ass eliminated," she said.

If Maria hadn't turned her back she would've saw the look Sin had and knew to get away. He slapped her down and went and opened her night stand drawer and grabbed her 9mm. Sin ejected the clip and cleared the chamber and put the clip and bullet in his pocket before Maria sat up. Sin pulled her up.

"You fuckin' trippin'!" she said with fear in her eyes.

"You wanna eliminate me? Here go the gun. Do it!" he said.

"No, I was just mad," she cried.

"Go on, take it and kill me," he said.

Maria started crying harder as she shook her head. "I don't wanna kill you!" she screamed. Sin felt bad because she was genuinely scared.

"Maria, you fucked us off," he said as he went in the bathroom. He slipped the clip back in and dropped the loose bullet back in the chamber. He walked out the bathroom and threw the gun on the bed on his way to the door.

"Don't go, Papi! We can do it," she said.

"It ain't even about that. I'll have Terell bring you the other $190,000," he said as he left. Maria smiled when she heard the door close.

"He passed my test," she said out loud. "But damn! Did he have to hit me that hard?" she said as she rubbed her cheek.

Chapter Eighteen

Air Out the Sin

I done fucked mine off again, Sin thought as he rode to downtown Oakland. When he got to 24 Hour Nautilus he parked in one of the lots across the street. He got out of the car and walked in and looked for Anita. When he found her, she had on some blue Nike tights, a blue Nike sports bra, and some white and blue Jordan's. Sin stood behind her looking at her ass for a minute. Anita must've felt him because she looked in the mirror and saw him.

"What're you doing?" she asked.

"Just admiring the view," he said. Anita got off the treadmill and wiped her face with a blue towel.

"Why you even come in here?" he asked seriously.

"I'm trying to lose a few pounds," she said.

"There's nothing wrong with you."

"My butt is too big," she said.

"Your butt is perfect," he said.

"I'll be ready after I shower," she said as she walked away.

Sin walked outside and called Shaunté.

"What's up, daddy?" she asked.

"Where you at?"

"I'm just getting to Sacramento."

"So, what's up, honey? You want to go on and jump the broom?" she asked.

"Don't play!"

"Nah, for real. I've been really thinking about it."

"Because you know I'm the perfect woman. I cook, I clean, I'll do what needs to be done, I got some good pussy *and* head, and I love you more than anyone else will," she said.

"So, yes or no?" he asked.

"I'll let you know. I have to think about it," she said.

"Bye!" Sin said and hung up.

●●●●●●

I can't believe he asked me to marry him! Shaunté thought as she pulled up to Déja's house in Berkeley. Déja's Camaro and Land Cruiser were in the driveway and Kenny's motorcycle was parked in front. Kenny was in love with Shaunté. She had broken down and given him some pussy a couple days after Sin pulled up on the turf with Sheree in the car. *Do I really wanna marry Sin?* she asked herself. *Hell muthafuckin yeah!*

"I'm going to go in here and tell Kenny it ain't cool for me to see him no more," she said as she got out of the Yukon.

●●●●●●

While Sin was standing outside the gym waiting on Anita, a cute chick caught his eye. She was light enough to pass for white except her pretty full lips prevented that. She had hazel brown eyes, long straight brown hair that came to the center of her back, and a very pretty face. She was 5'8" and weighed about 125 pounds. She had 32D titties, medium hips, sexy thighs, and a nice fat ass.

Sin smiled at her and she smiled back and motioned him over to her. He pushed away from the wall and walked over.

"Hi! I'm Tiara," she said. *Damn, he's cute,* she thought.

"I'm Simian," he said. *She damn near sounds white. I bet she's one of them "ain't no brotha good enough for me" type bitches,* he thought.

"I saw you standing there by yourself and wanted to tell you that you look good," she said.

"Thank you."

"Why don't you walk me to my car," she said.

"I don't know about all that, sweetheart. I'm kinda here with someone," he said.

"Is she your wife or girlfriend?" she asked.

"No, she's a friend."

"Then she shouldn't be upset."

Sin followed Tiara down the street to her car, which was a 1998 black BMW M3.

"So, Simian, what do you do?" she asked.

"I own five Top to Bottom Window, Carpet and Auto Detail Service in four cities," he lied.

"Oh, blue collar, huh?" she said disappointedly.

"I make good money."

"Well, thank you for walking me to my car," she said as she opened the door.

"Oh, it's like that now? What, because I don't wear suits to work everyday, I'm not good enough for you?" he asked.

Tiara sighed and said, "Baby, you look good and everything, but I need to be trying to get with someone who's on the same level I am. And no offense, but you you're not there yet."

"I'm willing to bet I made three times what you made last year," he said.

"Yeah, right. I'm Vice President for Bank of the West. I made every bit of $150,000," she said proudly.

"I made $500,000. We charge $250 per car. We do at a minimum 25 cars a day. Oh, and for the record, the only car I wash, and that's if I choose to, is my mine," he said arrogantly.

Tiara pulled a card out of her purse and wrote on the back. "Well, I apologize. Let me make it up to you. How about I take you to lunch?" she said.

"It ain't going to be cheap," he said.

"I wouldn't have it any other way," she said.

"Okay, I'll call you tomorrow," he said and walked away.

When Sin got back to the gym, Anita was coming out.

"We can go chill at my house. My address is 1445 8th Street, in Berkeley," she said as they walked over to a gold Camry.

"A'ight, I'll stop at the store and get some drank. You smoke?" he asked.

"For sure."

"I'll be there in thirty minutes," he said as he walked away. When Sin got to the Lexus, Tiara pulled up.

"Why don't you call me later on," she said.

"Okay, for sure, baby," he said. Tiara pulled off. *Your ass could've been more than just some pussy. After I beat that shit up and nut in your face I ain't never calling you,* he thought as he started the car and left.

Sin rode up to Shattuck and parked in the apartments on 46th. He went to Tessa's door and knocked.

"Who dat?" she yelled.

"Come open the door and see," he said. Tessa looked out

the window and saw Sin standing there. She opened the door and Sin walked in.

"You been out damn near four months and you just now coming to see me?" she asked with her hands on her hips. Tessa was about 5'9 and 130 pounds. She had medium length hair, gray eyes and milk chocolate colored skin. Her body was fucking over a video chicks. She had 34B cup titties, wide hips, a small waist, big sexy thighs, flat stomach, and a big sexy butt. She was wearing a T-shirt and some too small jeans.

"Tees, I ain't been trying to see nobody. I been trying to get my money right," he said.

"Nigga, we better than that. You acting like I'm a groupie or some shit," she said.

"It ain't like that. Now go on and sell me a 50 sack," he said. Tessa went to her freezer and grabbed a $50 bag of purple Kush.

He gave her the money and walked to the door. "Before I leave, turn around," he said. She turned and raised the back of her shirt and let him see the ass.

"Damn! My cousin Sha better be lucky he got you," Sin said as he left.

Sin got in the Lex and rode around the corner to the store. He ran in and purchased some Remy XO and saw Davy walking around the corner to make a sale. As he was coming out, He recognized the dude Davy was leading as Carlos. Carlos was a known jacker. Carlos had robbed Sin a few years ago for an ounce of rocks. Rod, June, and Sin caught up with him and stomped him unconscious and left him in some bushes on 43rd.

Carlos didn't try to retaliate because he knew he was outta pocket, and they knew where his family lived.

Sin put his purchases in the Lexus and grabbed his gun. He hurried around the corner saw them going between two houses. Sin heard voices coming from behind the two houses. He looked and saw Carlos had Davy at gunpoint.

"Man, you trippin'. When my bro find out about this shit, it's on!" Davy said.

"Nigga, I ain't about to tell you again. Empty your muthafuckin pockets or I'm gon' light you up and take it!" Carlos said. Davy gave him the $500 he had in his pocket and the two ounces of rocks.

"That watch and chain too," Carlos said. Davy gave it to him. Carlos backed away, and when he got to the front of the house he turned and Sin was right there with the Glock 40 pointed at his face.

"Throw the fuckin gun in the grass," Sin said.

"Man, why's you trippin' on me?" Carlos asked. Sin led him back between the houses.

"Man, your ass don't learn. Give my lil' bro his shit back!"

"Sin, I swear I didn't know he was your brother," he said as he took Davy's stuff out his pocket and gave it back to him.

"That's why I'm giving you a pass. You owe me, and I will be calling it in."

Davy looked at Sin crazy. “Fuck that, bro! Do this nigga!” he said as he put the watch back on.

Sin grabbed Davy’s dope and gave Carlos a 50. “When I need you, I’ll let your sister, Carmela, know,” Sin said as he and Davy left. When they got to the corner, Terell pulled up with his girl, LaVita.

“I need to re-up,” he said. Sin pulled his phone out and called Malika.

“Hello!” she said.

“I need you to do something for me,” he said.

“And what would that be, baby?” she asked in a sexy voice.

She must be smoking weed, he thought. “I’m fixing to have my potna come out there to KFC. I need you to take one of them things up there to him. B.G.’s coming too,” he said.

“Is he suppose to be giving me any money, and what time are you coming?” she asked.

“Seventeen-5, and I’ll be there before 2,” he said then gave her Terell’s mobile number and hung up.

“I’m gone,” he said. He went down the street and got in the Lexus and left.

When Sin got to Anita’s house, he realized she stayed around the corner from Déja. He got out of the car and went up the walkway. As he approached the door, Anita opened it wearing some red silk lounging pajamas. He walked in and immediately smelled weed.

"Come on," she said. He followed her to the backroom with his eyes glued to her ass.

"Have a seat and kick back," she said. He did and she handed him a blunt.

"This is a nice house," he said.

"It's a'ight," she said and took the bag and pulled the bottle out.

"XO, huh? What's the occasion?" she asked as she went to the bar and made their drinks.

"It ain't one. This is how we suppose to do it," he said.

"I bet you treat all the girls like this," she said as she came and sat down.

I do. That's why I'm always getting dogged. I'm too nice," he said.

"I can't see you allowing anyone to dog you," she said as she hit the weed again.

"Sweetheart, it happens. I'm no different from the next nigga. I done had my heart broken more times than the average man," he said.

Sin and Anita sat and talked for a few hours. Sin leaned over to her and kissed her. To Anita's surprise her lips parted as if they had a mind of their own, Sin stuck his thumbs in the waist of her pajama bottoms and pulled them down leaving her in the pajama top and red, silk French cut panties.

"What are you doing to me? I swear I don't usually get down like this," she said as he caressed her butt.

"That's why I'm going to stop," he said as he stood up.

"I didn't say I wanted you to stop," she said as she stood and kissed him.

"I know, but trust me, it would've led to other stuff and that ain't how I want it with you, feel me?" he asked.

"No, I don't feel you. How do you know that's not how I wanted it with you?" she asked.

"Shit, if that's the case I could've just went and got some E&J VSOP and met you at the marina and freaked you," he said.

"I don't know what I want," Anita sighed.

"I'm going to get out of here before I do some ol' freaky shit to you."

"Promises, promises," she said as she walked him outside to his car. Since her pajama top came down passed her butt she didn't worry about anything showing. They stood on the driver side of the Lex and kissed.

"Call me tomorrow," she said as she switched all the way back in the house.

As soon as Sin drove off, Anita went and dialed a number.

"Yeah!" the male answered.

"I don't think it's him," she said.

"Oh, it's him, and we gon' tear his punk ass out the frame," the voice replied.

"Whatever. I know one thing. Before we try to see this dude about something, we better be 100% ready, because he's going to come out busting, and I ain't fixing to be a casualty in your shit," she said and hung up.

Simian, I hope you ain't the one, she thought as she stood there hot and wet.

••••••

When Sin drove off, he knew he should've tapped that ass. He rode to the Shell gas station on Ashby and got some gas. While he stood there pumping, he called Malika.

"Hello!" she answered.

"I'll be there in a little while," he replied.

"Where are you?" she asked.

"In Berkeley getting gas."

"Oooohh, please bring me some ribs from Flint's," she asked.

"A'ight, I'll be there in a minute," he said and hung up.

Sin saw a black '82 Chev pull up. All of a sudden he got a

funny feeling. He hung the pump up and capped his tank. Sin's only thought was getting to his gun. He reached his door as all hell broke out. Two dudes jumped out of the Chev with their guns blazing. Sin felt the first bullet graze his neck. The next one hit him in the side, then one in the back. Sin fell into his car and that's when it got worse. The dudes lit the Lexus up. Sin got hit in the shoulder and the leg. He heard the Chev's doors slam and it pulled out leaving rubber.

As Sin lay there, he felt the life slipping from his body. *Fuck that! I ain't going out like that!* he thought. He heard sirens getting near, but then they started sounding as if they were going away. Sin's vision started going… *Malika, Tracy, Shaunte, Busy, Simara, Simina, Quesha, Mama…!*

The End, or maybe the beginning.

Street Knowledge!
"So Real You Think You've Lived It!"

Upcoming Novels From Street Knowledge Publishing

Coming 2007

The Hunger
By: Norman R. Colson

Shakers
By: Gregory D. Dixon

The Fold
By: Tehuti Atum-Ra

Time-Jack
By: John G. Whitfield

Dopesick 2
By: Sicily

Stackin' Paper
By: JoeJoe

Lust, Love, & Lies
By: Eric Fleming

No Other Love
By: Divine G

Dipped Up
By: Visa Rollack

Playin' For Keeps
By: Gregory Garrett

No Love-No Pain
By: Sicily

M.U.C.C.
By: Ronald Jackson

Dirty Livin'
By: Fernando Seirra

Street Knowledge Publishing Order Form

Street Knowledge Publishing, P.O. Box 345, Wilmington, DE 198
Email: jj@streetknowledgepublishing.com
Website: www.streetknowledgepublishing.com

For Inmates Orders and Manuscript Submissions
P.O. Box 310367, Jamaica, NY 11431

Bloody Money
ISBN # 0-9746199-0-6 **$15.00**
Shipping/ Handling Via
U.S. Priority Mail **$4.05**
Total **$19.05**

Me & My Girls
ISBN # 0-9746199-1-4 **$15.00**
Shipping/ Handling Via
U.S. Priority Mail **$4.05**
Total **$19.05**

Bloody Money 2
ISBN # 0-9746199-2-2 **$15.00**
Shipping/ Handling Via
U.S. Priority Mail **$4.05**
Total **$19.05**

Dopesick
ISBN # 0-9746199-4-9 **$15.00**
Shipping/ Handling Via
U.S. Priority Mail **$4.05**
Total **$19.05**

Money-Grip
ISBN # 0-9746199-3-0 **$15.00**
Shipping/ Handling Via
U.S. Priority Mail **$4.05**
Total **$19.05**

The Queen of New York
ISBN # 0-9746199-7-3 **$15.00**
Shipping/ Handling Via
U.S. Priority Mail **$4.05**
Total **$19.05**

Don't Mix The Bitter With The Sweet
ISBN # 0-9746199-6-5 **$15.00**
Shipping/ Handling Via
U.S. Priority Mail **$4.05**
To al **$19.05**

Street Knowledge Publishing Order Form

Page 2

Street Knowledge Publishing, P.O. Box 345, Wilmington, DE 19801
Email: jj@streetknowledgepublishing.com
Website: www.streetknowledgepublishing.com

Sin 4 Life
ISBN # 0-9746199-8-1 **$15.00**
Shipping/ Handling Via
U.S. Priority Mail **$4.05**
Total **$19.05**

The Hungry
ISBN # 0-9746199-5-7 **$15.00**
Shipping/ Handling Via
U.S. Priority Mail **$4.05**
Total **$19.05**

Stackin'PAPER
ISBN # 0-9755811-8-X **$15.00**
Shipping/ Handling Via
U.S. Priority Mail **$4.05**
Total **$19.05**

Purchaser Information

Name: ____

Address: ____

City: ___________State: ___Zip Code: ______________

Bloody Money ___

Me & My Girls ___

Bloody Money 2 ___

Dopesick ___

Money Grip ___

The Queen of New York ___

Don't Mix The Bitter With The Sweet ___

The Hungry ___

Sin 4 life ___

Stackin' PAPER ___

Quantity Of Books? ______

Make checks/money orders payable to:
Street Knowledge Publishing